Lost and Found

By Katerina Winters

Table of Contents

Contents

Chapter 1

Chapter 2

Chapter 3

Chapter 4

Chapter 5

Chapter 6

Chapter 7

Chapter 8

Chapter 9

Chapter 10

Chapter 11

Chapter 12

Chapter 13

Chapter 14

Chapter 15

Chapter 16

Chapter 17

Chapter 18

Chapter 19

Chapter 20

Chapter 21

Chapter 22

Chapter 23

Chapter 24

Chapter 1

Just as always the girl with the one ear was waiting for him. Mikhail Kulakov, one of Boston's two main Russian mob bosses, was quite intrigued by the wide-eyed girl. For a couple of months now he has been visiting Milly's Diner for his morning coffee. Milly's was not only under his jurisdiction, but they also made the best blueberry scones in Boston. However, for the past few weeks he has been stopping by for more than just his sweet tooth.

The girl was no more that eight or nine, Mikhail surmised, she always wore the same outfit. A pair of too short jeans with flower embroidery, man-sized construction gloves, and a threadbare badly stained blue scarf. But her most recognizable piece of clothing was a small black puff jacket that rode high on her wrist. The jacket stood out the most, due to the fact that it had Mickey Mouse ears, or at least it had more than one ear at one time in its life. All the clues pointed to one obvious conclusion—she was homeless.

"Dobroye utro Mikhail." she sat on the curb near his black BMW with a large smile.

Holding his coffee along with a brown paper bag with his scones, he walked over to his car sliding into the front seat. As was his routine he rolled down the window and waited for her to come closer.

"Kak dela?" he responded in his mother tongue, watching the large brown eyes scrunch in thought as she carefully tried to come up with a response.

"khor...khora...no no wait it's khoro." by now she was desperate to get it right. Mikhail smirked while taking a sip of his coffee waiting to see if she could grasp the elusive word. "KHOROSHIY!"

"Good. Your pronunciation has improved a bit from last time," he said with an approving nod as he pulled out one of the two scones. Mikhail knew from experience that offering her a scone would only result in her polite refusal so he tried a new tactic. "I will trade you this scone for one of your hand warmers."

Her smile grew larger as she held the box she had been holding higher to his open window. Shifting her weight he watched her balance the box with one hand as she used her teeth to pull off the large work glove. Mikhail watched the surprisingly tiny hand slip from the giant dirty glove and hand him the warmers he really didn't want.

Tossing the warmers in the seat next to him, he handed her the scone.

"Thank you," he watched with veiled interest as she hungrily devoured her scone. Absently he handed her one of his restaurant napkins he had laying in the car. The Rose was the restaurant he owned, located in the industrial side of town, but on the edge of the up and coming art district. After his morning meeting with the little urchin, he would join his captains for morning meetings in the back room at the Rose. As if catching herself for showing her hunger, she sheepishly looked down while changing subjects. "I looked up some information about the tattoos on your forearm.

"And what did you find?" he sipped his coffee while checking his phone for messages.

"Well I only saw a couple tattoos, but it seems like your pretty high ranking in your organization." When he didn't answer she continued, "I found the information online at the library, the same time I listened to the Russian beginner videos."

The fascination she had with his tattoos reminded him of how he first met her. It was one of the few days he let one of his men drive him to the office. Mikhail was surrounded by his men practically day and night he enjoyed an occasional drive by himself. But it simply wasn't done, to have the boss without protection was ludicrous, that's why Nico, one of Krill's boys drove him that morning. Sending Nico out to pick up his order Mikhail sat in the backseat of the black SUV and answered emails. Out of the corner of his eye, he watched the little girl get closer and closer to the vehicle. The black tinted windows kept her from seeing in, but that didn't seem to stop her. Holding a large dented box, she shuffled closer and closer until she was right beside his door.

The loud knock on his window ruined his intention to ignore the encroaching girl. Sighing he pressed the button to lower the window.

"Sorry to bother you sir, I just wanted to know if you would like to buy some hand warmers for two dollars." A red packet was already through the window, dangling from her gloved hand.

Her boldness was shocking and a little amusing. Mikhail couldn't remember the last time someone was so bold. Turning his head, he looked down to get a better look at who exactly was sticking their hand in the car of a criminal.

Big brown eyes stared up at him expectantly as she held the warmers out, her light brown skin was slightly red due to the below freezing winds. From the little hair he could see around the tightly synched hood it looked to be wavy jet black hair. Her small slightly upturned nose was covered in small freckles. The large smile she offered was all teeth, which were surprisingly white considering her lack of a home. But it was her eyes that drew his attention, they were huge. Large innocent brown eyes full of hopeful happiness, despite her current situation.

"No thank you," a brief flash of disappointment went across the vivid eyes but was quickly replaced with curiosity.

Though she withdrew her hand, she remained in the same spot. "I like your accent. It's not German and it's not French. But judging by your driver, the neighborhood, and your tattoos on you knuckles I say Russian." when he didn't answer immediately, doubt settled in. "Am I wrong? I'm sorry. I have been reading detective books and I have been trying to notice more stuff like the detec..."

"Your right." He had to stop her before she went on any further. It was evident that she didn't talk to many people. Though he was surprised by her aptitude, Mikhail never hung around too many children but he would hazard a guess that she was quite sharp for her age. "What's your name?"

For the first time during their conversation, a hint of wariness came over her. It seemed the age old adage of don't talk to strangers was beginning to filter through.

"Misha," she began hesitantly, "Misha Abosi. What's yours?"

"Mikhail Kulakov." Her waning smile returned full force as he pronounced his name. She repeated it a couple of times, seemingly liking the sound of it.

"I like your tattoos. Do they mean something?" Mikhail wasn't sure how to respond to such an abrupt change in subject, not to mention such a dangerous topic. However, Nico's return saved him from responding to the innocent question.

"Aye! Get out of here!" the harsh yell from his driver startled the small urchin. The cheery face was replaced by a brief note of fear. Just as quickly as she appeared she left, Mikhail watched the one-eared coat disappear around the neighboring building.

Rolling up his window he waited for Nico to begin driving.

"Nico."

"Yes sir?" he could see the man's awaiting eyes though the rear view mirror. Nico was actually a couple of years older than Mikhail. His hair was slightly longer than it should be, along with his seemingly permanent five-o-clock shadow Nico always seemed to have a casual look.

"Don't ever interrupt me like that again." Mikhail made sure to make eye contact with the enforcer. He wanted to make sure Nico could see his cold displeasure.

"Of course sir," a shadow of fear that crossed Nico's face, just as the one he caused on Misha.

Since that day, he has made it a point to see the urchin every day. With every passing morning, she became more comfortable around him, even with Nico who she wrangled into buying some warmers once.

"Tomorrow lets see how far you get with your Russian." As usual his promise to see her the following morning made her smile brighter.

"Bye Mikhail, see you tomorrow," she chirped before backing away from the starting car. As he pulled away, he watched her out of his rear view mirror. The one-eared girl vigilantly stood there watching his black car disappear.

Early the next morning, Mikhail was greeted by Nico when he stepped off the elevator in his condo.

"Hello sir." wearing his usual all black suit and black gloves, Nico stepped forward to take his briefcase.

Mikhail grunted in response. He was not pleased, but it was pointless to send him back since they were going to the same location. After his customary morning meeting at The Rose, Mikhail went to his office in the shipyards. Since Nico actually worked in one of the warehouses as a foreman, it made no sense to demand the man to leave.

It was still very early in the morning, looking out his window into the dark early morning sky Mikhail let his thought drift to Misha again. Where did she sleep? Where were her parents?

Passing under the main overpass that was near Milly's, Mikhail noticed the flashing lights of police and ambulance. Though there weren't many cars this early in the morning, the traffic through the intersection slowed considerably due to curious onlookers.

"Don't worry sir, I will get you there in time." After weaving through the clogged traffic, Nico got them back on track allowing them to arrive only a minute past his normal time.

Misha wasn't there. The familiar one ear jacket was nowhere in sight. A cold feeling formed in the pit of Mikhail's stomach, Misha was never late.

Nico got out to go get his order, but with each minute that passed and no sighting from his usual greeter, the feeling in the pit of his stomach grew colder. The rush of cold air swirled into the SUV as Nico climbed back into the driver seat.

"Sir I thought you should know, the scene down the block was from a stabbing," Nico said quietly as handed him the coffee. Nico must have noticed Misha's unusual absence. Catching the dark look in his eyes, Nico quickly added, "It was an older male transient."

After waiting an extra twenty minutes, he ordered Nico to drive to the restaurant. A part of him was angry that the little street urchin stood him up. Mikhail should have probably felt foolish for waiting, but another part of him was consumed with the cold gut feeling that something was wrong. Mikhail could sense Nico's restlessness as well.

Pulling up to The Rose, Mikhail slowly got out, with every mile his agitation grew. Shutting the door, he walked to the driver's window.

"Nico, I want you to go back the scene and find out more info." With a quick nod Nico drove away.

For a moment Mikhail stood there, there weren't too many times he felt this type of inability. He had no way of contacting her nor did he know where she slept. Even though his pride would take some damage he couldn't help but hope she stood him up.

Chapter 2

Sitting at his usual table in the back of The Rose, Mikhail absently listened to Abram drone on about the new car one of his boys picked up. Abram Zharkov was Mikhail's second captain, he ran a massive chop shop discreetly hidden outside the city. Abram was a thirty-five year old chronic smoker, gambling, pot head who looked nineteen. He had a full set of pearly white teeth that were bigger than they should have been compared to his mouth. Abram was always laughing and smoking, even when he was killing a man. Since the day Mikhail picked his captain up from the GULAG mining labor camp, the captain lived his life with abandon. The only two things to be counted on from Abram was his unwavering loyalty to Mikhail and his uncanny ability to make money.

Earlier that night Nico finally got back to him with the information he requested. A homeless man was stabbed to death near the Davis overpass. He was found under the bridge by another transient. Using some of their resources in the local police department, Nico found the man's priors: robbery, vandalism, loitering, and numerous cases of sexual assault.

Mikhail remained stoic as usual towards his soldier's report, but his mind was racing. The feeling in his gut remained the same as the morning, something was not right. Ignoring Abram's rants Mikhail decided that if Misha were not in her normal spot tomorrow morning he would send some men to look for her. At this point he didn't care what his men may think of his interest in the child, Mikhail needed to know.

"Boss!" a shout from the back hallway hushed the entire back room. Everyone went still, alert and ready. The source of the voice Michael, a young man that worked in his shipyards, came running in.

The expression on his face was of a confused shock. "Sir you might want to come see this."

The moment he stood up, Abram stood up right beside him, as expected the captain followed Mikhail as he made his way down the back hallway. Everyone else in the private back room remained seated but stayed quiet, for a chance to hear what was going on. Reaching the back alley metal door, that was being held open by two more of his crew all wearing the same confused expression.

"What the hell is going on?" Mikhail's demanded sharply. The small group of men standing in the alley stood aside to reveal a blood soaked child.

"Misha!" Mikhail's eyes widened as he stared at her. Misha was wearing her normal clothing, but nothing else was normal about her. Even in the dark back alley Misha's coat and jeans were visibly coated in blood. Her usual smiling face was frozen in a look of shock. In her hand she held what looked to be a blood-soaked box cutter.

Leaning close to him Michael whispered in his ear, "We were all out here smoking when she came up to us. She asked for you by name and gave us this." Mikhail took the bloodstained item from Michael.

It was the napkin he gave her the other morning with the restaurant's logo and address.

"Misha." slowly he stepped forward from the door so she could see him. The sound of his voice seemed to break the trance she was in. "Misha, what happened?"

"Mikhail," she whispered softly, the large eyes that were staring blankly focused on him. "woke up and he was on top of me. He broke my jacket and tore my pants."

Everyone remained silent as they tried to decipher her broken words.

"I just kept stabbing him." by now her voice was getting louder and she was no longer looking at him, her eyes were glazed over as she recalled the events. "I don't want to go to jail," the words came out as a desperate plea.

Mikhail sensed everyone bristle at her last words. All of his men were ex-convicts, each one of them would rather die than go back to prison. It was one of the main reasons why he handpicked each one of them. Crushing the napkin in his fist realizing she must have walked from Milly's to find him made his blood boil, he should have listened to his instinct earlier.

"Misha come here," he stepped closer to her, he needed to see if any of the blood was hers. When he stepped forward Abram and the other men followed suit. Immediately he recognized their mistake, still clutching the bloody box cutter she realized she was being surrounded by his men. Fear quickly took over. Instinctively she tried to back away from the group.

"Wait!" Mikhail barked the order to Michael, who was trying to grab her. But Michael's clumsy attempt to grab her was enough to spook her. With a quickness only a child could have, she dodged his men and took off towards the street.

"Misha wait!" he ran after her, closing in on her he was only a few yards away from catching up. The pounding feet on pavement told him his men were not far behind. But she reached the mouth of the alley before he could. She didn't see the car backing up, nor did the driver see her. Mikhail watched in horror as the car hit the one eared girl.

Quickly he skid to a halt next to her body, kneeling beside her he slowly turned her over. A female scream and the curses of his men vaguely registered in his mind. Abram yelled to his men to get Isaac, their personal doctor. Mikhail was relieved to see she was still breathing. The car only seemed to hit her on the shoulder, knocking her to the ground, from what he could tell nothing was broken.

"Take care of the driver." Mikhail didn't need to see if Abram heard his order, he could already hear him yelling at the driver to get out.

Picking up the little girl, Mikhail noticed that she still was clutching the box cutter.

Isaac meet them at Mikhail's condo. It was an older high rise building Mikhail owned in an up and coming neighborhood. It was one of the first investments he made when he came to America. It took every penny he had to buy the place, thankfully the investment paid off well. By now he could have bought another place, a newer place even, but this one was his trophy it reminded him how far he came.

Taking the private elevator to the penthouse Mikhail carried Misha's unconscious body to one of the four empty spare bedrooms. Laying her on the bare twin sized bed, that just happen to come with the condo, he stepped back so Isaac could take a look.

Stepping out into the hall Abram walked up to him. "Sir, I took care of the driver, he thinks he hit a stray dog." Abram winced apologetically when he noticed Mikhail's acrid glare before continuing, "I made sure any witnesses were given free drinks to help with any memory problems. And I had Vera stop by."

Vera Domoshev was one of the strippers that worked at Krill's club, when she wasn't working at the club she worked at The Rose. She was the only women Mikhail halfway trusted, unlike all the other vapid money hungry women who worked for Krill she was the only one that had a head for the business.

"Good." Mikhail walked back into the room to see that Isaac had taken off Misha's jacket and scarf. It was the first time Mikhail seen her without the tightly synched one-eared hood. Looking at her skinny body he wondered how long she had been on the streets. It must have not been too long if her pride could still let her turn down free food, he wondered.

"Oh, that poor thing." Vera made her entrance by ignoring both men as she swept past them to kneel next to the doctor. "Is she ok?" she looked at Isaac expectantly.

"Dammit Vera let the man finish." Abram's command went unheeded as Vera looked at Mikhail.

"Mikhail, I heard what happened from Michael. Do you think Isaac or I should check to see if, you know..."she paused but she gave him a meaningful look as she gestured towards Misha's torn pants.

Holding back the sickening rage that sprang forth he grunted his approval and stepped out of the room, shutting the door on Vera and Isaac. Needing a drink, he made his way to the kitchen with Abram in tow.

Silently he fixed himself and Abram a whiskey. Normally Mikhail was not a talker, he really didn't have to be with his two captains. Krill and Abram were the most talkative men Mikhail had ever met. But even Abram was quiet now as they waited for the Isaac's report. Mikhail knew Abram had questions about Misha, but Mikhail also knew Abram was smart enough to be patient.

Finally after what felt like an eternity, Isaac walked into the kitchen.

"The girl is fine, just a slight concussion, she was able to wake up and seems fully cognizant." Taking a sip of the offered whiskey Abram handed him, he continued. "And there were no signs of sexual abuse, just a couple of bruises from the attack. Vera is with her now getting her cleaned up."

"I'll show the doctor out." Abram offered.

Walking to his room Mikhail grabbed a couple of shirts. Outside of the occupied guestroom he could hear the soft feminine voices through the door, knocking softly he waited.

Opening the door wide enough to stick her head through Vera eyed him carefully.

"I brought some shirts." Silently she took the shirts and closed the door.

Taking the cue he wasn't needed he went to his living room. Mikhail rarely used his living room, he spent all day working at his office in the shipyards and all night with his captains catching up with the other various business. Out of the two Russian organizations in Boston Mikhail's was the most legit, the other was Roman Mashir. Roman was as dirty and typical as they came. The man was into anything illegal from prostitution, guns, drugs, kidnappings, you name it and Roman was in the thick of it. Roman lost more men per month than Mikhail could count. Mikhail on the other hand ran a much more quiet profitable organization. Both he and Roman worked for Vladimir, the leading vory of Russia.

"So you gonna tell me?" Abram's playful voice interrupted his thoughts.

Not turning his head Mikhail continued to stare out at the city skyline. "I met the kid while getting coffee at Milly's."

Silence permeated the air.

Abram must have realized he wasn't going to divulge any further, so he changed topics. They began discussing the next shipment of cars when Vera came in to sit next to Abram, holding a pile of Misha's dirty clothes.

"Well I got her cleaned up and dressed but," she paused, shifting the pile of clothes in her hands. "what do you want to do with these? I have a couple of things at my place I could bring over that might fit her. But she will need some other things." she lifted one of her sculpted eyebrows pointedly at him.

Grabbing his wallet from his pocket, Mikhail pulled out a handful of hundred dollar bills. "Here get the kid what she needs." Mikhail handed the money to Vera, ignoring both her and Abram's wide eye expressions. "And burn that." Pointing to the pile of blood-soaked clothes.

"How much should I get, I mean if she is going back to the streets or even to foster care she won't be able to..."

"Don't worry about that," Mikhail cut her off harshly, "Just get her the stuff. After she recovers I will think about what to do with her." Getting up, he walked to his bedroom, silently signaling them to leave.

The simultaneous "Yes sir." as they hurried out the last thing he heard.

Sighing Mikhail sat at the edge of his bed later on that night, and reflected on the day's events. He was angry with himself for ignoring his intuition. Moreover he was confused by his actions. Why in the hell did he take the kid into his home? Why did he care what happened to the kid? He wasn't sure if he saw a little bit of himself in her, watching her struggle to survive, brought back the bone chilling childhood memories. Whatever it was it didn't answer the current question, what the hell was he going to do with her now?

Chapter 3

Misha awoke with a start, the image of that man trying to touch her plagued her dreams. Looking around she started to panic. The bare white walls of the room at first reminded her of the stories she read on asylums and prisons, though the large floor to ceiling windows seemed out of place in that possibility. Trying hard, she tried to remember what happened. Misha remembered finding Mikhail, she remembered getting scared at all those men staring at her and running, and she remembered the nice brown haired lady.

Taking a deep breath she sighed, she remembered now, Vera told her she was in Mikhail's home. Vera was so nice, she helped her wash her hair and change into the large clean shirt. Looking down Misha grabbed the collar of the shirt and brought it to her nose. It smelled nice. Getting off the bed she walked to the connecting bathroom. As she used the toilet she smiled, it was so nice being able to use the bathroom in an actual bathroom or without getting stern looks from the librarian.

Though she couldn't see her entire reflection due to the counter Misha was shocked by the image. She had not seen her hair washed and loose in what seemed like forever. But Misha knew, she knew exactly how many months and days it had been when she was dropped off. Fighting back tears she walked back into the bedroom and edged closer to the door.

Pressing her ear to the door Misha strained to hear anything from the other side. Vera told her to not leave the room, that she was to wait until she gets there. Vera said Mikhail was very particular and that she didn't want her to get in trouble. Backing away from the door, Misha sat back on the bed and brought her knees to her chest underneath the large shirt.

A light quick knock on the door startled her awake, she must have dozed off and didn't realize it. Before Misha could answer, Vera swept in closing the door behind her. The tall brown haired lady wore the same comforting smile as she did the night before, but this time her hands were full of bags.

"Good your awake. How do you feel?" Misha didn't get a chance to respond, Vera was already plopping down on the bed beside her, "I got you some stuff, thanks to Mikhail of course."

Misha wanted to protest, she didn't want Mikhail to give her any more than she already got, but Vera was like a tornado. She was being undressed and dressed before she could say or do anything. And Misha really liked the exciting lady, she was really nice to her. Occasionally agreeing or smiling at Vera's conversation Misha got a better look at the woman. Vera had long straight brown hair, it was the kind of silky hair Misha had seen on commercials, the kind of hair Misha wish she had, instead her hair was big and curly. She wore knee high black boots that were super tall with polka dot leggings, a skirt, and sweater. Misha thought she looked like a Barbie doll, with her blue eyes and bright red lips.

"There you are." Holding Misha by the shoulders Vera admired her work. "Here come take a look." Prompting her to stand on the rim of the tub, Misha was now able to see most of herself in the bathroom mirror.

Misha smiled at the sight of her new jeans and sweater, but what she really liked were the black furry boots. Unlike her old boots, they gave her toes plenty of wiggle space.

"Thank you so much," she was hugging Vera before she realized it. Quickly she stepped back, "I'm sorry."

"Don't apologize," Vera hugged her back to prove it. "Oh I also got you a suitcase to put all your stuff in." Vera pointed to the pink kitty suitcase in the corner.

The sight of the suitcase reminded her of the plastic bag of personal belongings she kept under the bridge near Millys. It would be a crime to put that dirty bag into that pretty case. Misha would have to find somewhere else to sleep from now on, she couldn't go back to that spot. Not after what happened. Instinctively she went to put her hands in her pocket to clutch the box cutter she kept close. But when she didn't find it she realized again where she was. Looking up she saw the sad look cross over Vera's face, she must have noticed her zoning out. Giving her the biggest smile Misha tried to forget about the uncertain future and the past.

"Come on let's show Mikhail." Vera grabbed her hand and led her out of the room. Misha's heart beat nervously as she followed her down the empty hallway. Just like her room, everything she could see was either white or gray. There were no pictures or anything on the walls. Reaching the kitchen she stopped as she was now face to face with the man who visited her every morning.

Mikhail casually leaned against the kitchen counter reading his emails, the footsteps brought his attention up from his phone. Blinking a couple of times he couldn't believe the transformation.

"Ta da." Ignoring Vera's usual flare for dramatics he stared at the wide-eyed girl standing next to her. Hair and lots of it was the first thing he noticed. Long puffy black curls framed her face like a lion's mane. All the hair accompanying her huge eyes, kinda made him want to laugh—but he refrained. Her nervous smile brought him back to reality.

"Privetstvovat." His welcoming greeting seemed to take away the nervousness.

Misha did her best to pronounce the Russian "thank you" in return, she loved hearing Mikhail's voice. His heavy accented English was super deep, but his Russian was somehow deeper. Misha remembered the first time she saw him through his SUV window. He looked young but very stern, his nose was kind of big like a Roman statue, the muscles in his jaw looked quite strong hollowing slightly near his mouth. She couldn't tell what color his hair was by the hair on his head, because there wasn't hardly any left. All his hair was shaved off leaving only a whisper of growing hair. But judging by his eyebrows she would say his hair was light brown. Although out of all his features, it was the icy blue eyes she liked the most, she never seen eyes so blue before.

Icy blue eyes that were staring at her. While Vera was talking about what she purchased and how there was no change due to how expensive everything was nowadays, he was staring directly at her. Unsure of how to respond Misha smiled bigger. That seemed to snap him out of it.

"Yeah whatever Vera, keep the change," his tone suggested he was done talking about the matter.

Vera brightened at the answer and turned to her. "Ok sweety I will see you soon." with a quick hug Vera was already making her way to what Misha assumed was the front door. Panic started to set in. Misha didn't know what to do? She didn't want Vera to go. What if she did something wrong and Mikhail got angry? Not knowing what to do she turned back to Mikhail.

"Come here Misha," walking the living room Mikhail sat down on the large gray couch. Taking the matching smaller sofa to the side she sat at the edge.

"Where are your parents?" he asked slowly. Leaning forward with both elbows on his knees while he balanced his chin on the flat of his knuckles he patiently waited.

It's not like she didn't know this question was coming, Misha knew that he deserved an answer for all that he done for her already. But the pain of remembering threatened to bring tears. She did not want to cry, especially not in front of him. Having him think she was some crybaby would make him regret taking her in. She did not want to risk that, taking a deep breath she tried to push back the stinging feeling in the back of her throat.

"My mom," she started slowly, "left me. She left me in front of the diner two months and seven days ago." not wanting to look at him she focused on the circular pattern in the rug as she continued. "She said she was going to take my brothers and sisters to the doctor and I could go to the library and wait in the diner until she was done. She even gave me twenty dollars since it was my birthday. I bought a milkshake." even thinking about it now she wished she would have saved that money spent on that shake.

Silence permeated the air between them. Nervously Misha started to fiddle with her jeans as she waited for him to say something.

"Your mother is a bitch." the harsh words were spoken in such a deep low tone, she snapped her head up meeting his glacial gaze directly. As usual his face was emotionless, Misha wasn't sure how she was supposed to react.

The smile spread across her lips before she could stop it. For some reason all Misha wanted to do was cry and laugh. Yes that exactly what she was—a bitch. She would never say that out loud of course, but she would think it.

Mikhail, satisfied with her response, stood up and walked to the large wall of windows. "You can stay here until your fully recovered and then," he paused to turn to look at her. Misha held her breath for his next words, "we will figure out what to do next."

A relief washed over her, taking away any of the energy she had with it, tiredly but happily she smiled at him. She was so grateful to him, she had to tell him how much this meant to her. But before she could say anything he was grabbing his keys off the counter walking towards the door.

"I am leaving, I will send Krill to bring you food," seeing her worried look he pressed on, "I trust Krill with my life besides I am sure you will like him." With that he was gone.

Chapter 4

Misha couldn't decide who she loved more, Krill or Mikhail. Krill Burak was the funniest nicest man she ever met. He was a little shorter than Mikhail but much thicker than him. Not so much fat but more of just a really big man. Krill reminded her of a greco roman wrestler. His hair was black and shiny as well as his goatee. The first day they meet, they went to a Chinese Buffet. They both got so full, she thought she was going to get sick. He told her stories of Russia, showed her the clubs he owned and even showed her where Mikhail worked. By the time he escorted her back to Mikhail's house, it was night time.

Seeing the building for the first time from the outside, Misha admired the clean lobby area and the concierge desk. Behind the desk was a tall red headed woman. Misha smiled at her, but she didn't smile back. Taking the elevator, Krill showed her what buttons to press to get to Mikhail's floor.

By the time Krill left she was too tired to move. Laying down that night she couldn't help but the thank God she met Mikhail, even if she was back on the streets the next day she would still be happy for the moment of happiness she got to enjoy today.

Weeks passed by from the day she was taken in, her status was still unknown. Every morning she would wake up only to say her morning Russian greetings to Mikhail. Every morning they added a little more to the conversation, but not much. Once he finished his coffee at the kitchen counter, he would grab his keys and walk out the door. Even though his was a very distant man, Misha still loved her morning chats the most. However most of the time, Misha made sure to stay out of his way. Partly she didn't want to become a nuisance reminding him that he only said she would stay until she recovered and another part of her stayed away because she wasn't sure if he liked her all that much.

Every day his face seemed to harden a little more when he saw her. Misha would catch his icy blue stare, he looked as if he was confused and angry. Misha tried asking Krill and Vera, but they both waved her worries off with a smile. Always saying that, "That's just how he is," or "Don't worry he always looks that way."

Misha didn't think so, worry started to settle in the back of her mind.

Stepping off the elevator Mikhail unlocked the front door, as usual the place was only lit by the city lights coming in from the large wall of windows, as if there was nobody home. Sighing, he flipped on the living room light, no matter what he did he couldn't get Misha to stop tip-toeing around him. Mikhail had his weekly housekeeper add more food to his grocery delivery, but only a few bits of food were actual eaten. He had to actually tell Misha to eat more than just a handful of food.

Walking towards the kitchen he glanced down the hallway that led to the guest bedrooms. The old mid-century condo was almost perfect for their situation, the long unit had the master bedroom down a hallway to the left of the front door and the guest rooms on the other side, separated by the living area and kitchen. Unfortunately, it wasn't quite perfect.

He was forced adjust his usual sexual activities due to his new setup. First thing next week he was having some of his men install a soundproof sliding pocket door to the hallway leading to his bedroom. And due to Krill's persistence Misha was getting a change of scenery starting Monday as well. Seeing the light beneath her door, Mikhail began to knock but realized when he got closer the door was slightly open.

Leaning against the wall while sitting on her bed, Misha was reading a book she most likely got from the library with Krill. Wearing a pink pajama set and her curly black hair in a ponytail she forced him to ask himself for the millionth time—why the hell was he doing this?

Every time he looked at her he asked that question, and in turn that question made him angry. Since the night he took her home from the club, word spread amongst his men about the boss's new toy. Krill and Abram laid down an iron fist to make sure the foul rumor didn't spread outside of their organization, but they couldn't stop the internal gossip.

Both of his captain's had well over forty soldiers to their crew, each man pledged their loyalty to the captains and their life to Mikhail. Their organization was special, each man was hand picked. Mikhail offered them a chance at wealth and assurance. A peace of mind that they would never go back to the GULAG camp they were picked up from. Translated it meant Main Administration of Corrective Labor Camps and Labor Settlements, never again would they be subjected to their country's cruelty. Each one was directly transported from the camp and given the choice to either work for Roman Mashir, a promise of an exciting short life full of guns, women, and killing that would quickly lead to them either dying or being drug back to Russia. The other option was to swear their life to Mikhail, serve him without question, and have the peace of mind they never once had before. But even with his men devout loyalty they were still thugs, who thought like scum and gossiped like bitches.

Doing his best to clear his mind of his current problem he stepped forward into the small room. Taking notice of his presence, she clapped her book close with a large smile.

"Hi Mikhail," her excitement was audible, he normally didn't see her at night. "How was your day?"

"My day was the same as always. I have something for you," stepping forward he handed her the documents in his hand. He waited for her to open them before continuing, "I found your birth certificate and other government papers. I had a man of mine change a few necessary things," her eyes widened at the implication. "From this day forward until I change my mind, you are technically adopted by Krill. And starting Monday you will be going to school." Her reaction was not what he expected.

A watery sheen appeared in her wide eyes, for a second he feared she would start crying. Thankfully nothing came of the moisture, she just sat there staring at her papers. Finally after what seemed like minutes she looked up at him. "I love you."

The unspeakable childhood he endured, the short time in a mining camp in the mountains in Russia, even to his introduction to Vladamir's crew none of these things prepared him for the shock her words caused. Unsure of what his response should be, he turned and left.

Hours later he laid in bed staring out of the windows in his room. Absently he watched the blinking red lights of a plane cross the darkened sky. In that moment, he came to terms with his decision. Mikhail now knew why he kept the strange kid. Frankly he just liked her. Life had gotten monotonous, even as a crime boss his life had become prosaic. It was partly due to the fact that he ran his sector of the organization the smartest which in turn led it to be the safest, but that was neither here nor there.

Misha was like a shining light. For him their morning talks were therapeutic, it was the first time in years he looked forward to something. And he be damned if the idle gossip of his men were going to destroy that.

Krill, Abram, and Mikhail sat in the kitchen as Mikhail washed the blood off his hands. Today both of his captains witnessed Mikhail's savage anger. It had been years since the last time either of the captains seen Mikhail react in such violence, he was normally so cool and methodical.

They were all supposed to meet at the shipyard office instead of the restaurant since Krill wanted to be at Mikhail's home by four. Judging, by the way, Krill talked about the kid all the time, Abram was sure it had something to do with the kid's first day at school.

Unfortunately, Abram had some more pressing news to tell before they could get down to their usual talk of business.

Since the day he met Mikhail Kulakov, Abram had great respect for the young man, the despite their over sixteen year age difference. Every promise of wealth and freedom Mikhail made, Abram received in spades. Any enemy that Abram made Mikhail was always right there by his side. So when he heard some of his men talking in the back of his shop about Mikhail and some of the things he was probably doing to his new "pet," Abram made sure to tell Mikhail first thing.

The words were barely out of his mouth before Mikhail shot out of his chair. Without a word Mikhail left his office causing both Abram and Krill to run after him to catch up. The drive to Abram's shop was fast and silent. Slamming the car in park Mikhail hopped out of the black Beamer with each captain hot on his trail. When they found the main guy doing the most talking, Abram wasn't sure why he expected a simple threatening conversation, hell Mikhail didn't even say anything.

Walking directly to the man underneath the car Mikhail bent down and grabbed the protruding ankle, in one swift violent tug Mikhail hauled the man from beneath the vehicle. The man's shouts went unheeded as Abram's entire shop watched in silence at the violent scene. Picking the man up like a rag doll Mikhail slammed the man's head against the open hood of the car. Turning the stunned man over Mikhail began to punch him in the face until the dead weight of the unconscious man forced his body to slip away from Mikhail's grip. Standing over the bloody, unconscious man, his once white shirt sprayed with blood Mikhail looked calmly around the garage to his stunned audience.

"Does anyone else have something to say about me?" the deep voice was surprisingly calm. Men shaking their heads and occasional 'No sir' filtered the air.

With a brusque nod Mikhail walked away.

Still in his bloody shirt, Mikhail had his back to them as he washed his hands at the kitchen sink when they heard the door open. Simultaneously the three men turned their head to see a red blur whiz through the living room. Stopping in front of them, Misha gave off her brightest smile. Dressed in her new wool red coat and matching hat, she was the picture of innocence.

"Misha my darling! How was school?" Abram wanted to roll his eyes at Krill's adoration, but he just watched as he hugged the kid.

"It was great! I meet lots of nice girls, they even have an after school music program..." her words trailed off as she noticed the blood on Mikhail's shirt. "What happened?"

Abram watched with the greatest of interest as Mikhail looked down at his new roommate. Toweling off his scraped knuckles he sat down at one of the bar stools. "What's with the note?" he motioned at the white envelope pinned to her jacket.

Seemingly moving on from the bloody shirt she responded "Oh it's for Krill from my teacher." Krill unpinned the note and read it.

"It says they're moving her from third grade to fifth grade." His large proud smile made Abram want to puke. "My angel is so smart. Look at this." Thrusting the paper into Abram's face.

"Yes dammit I heard you," Abram yelled, swiping the paper away.

While chatting about her day to the silent listening crowd, Misha quickly made a plate of food. Grabbing her bag and plate Misha excused herself from the kitchen to go to her room. Mikhail smirked at the kid's mindfulness, he was happy that she could figure out when her presence was not needed. Though he couldn't quite say the same for Krill, who was still gushing over her advancement. Wiping the last of the blood from his forearm, he reflected on his thoughts last night. Yes he made a good decision.

Chapter 5

Misha couldn't hardly wait for the thick metal door that quarantined Mikhail's side to slide open. The small gourmet cake was all ready to go, the balloons were delicately tied to the present she was going to give him. The bright blue wrapping paper shielded, what she thought was her best gift to date.

With a familiar whoosh the door opened and as usual a tall skinny pouty blond walked through, stomping towards the front door. Misha learned long ago to ignore his multitude of trampy dates. No matter how many times she used to wave or smile, every single one looked at her with pure hatred. At first she thought it was just egoism, but the more she thought about it she thought it might have something to do with the fact they were kicked out unceremoniously so early in the morning. But Misha didn't care or at least she stopped caring, this was her time with Mikhail. From the moment their friendship formed, mornings have been their bonding hour. Well as much as one could bond with the tall, stoic mob boss.

"I am giving you ten minutes to put your clothes on," she yelled brightly down the hallway. Running back to the kitchen she scooped up her cake and present.

Walking into his room always gave her a rush. When she was younger, she was never allowed in the room, but as she got older she got a little bolder. At first she started out by simply following him while chatting about school, as time went by she would casually sneak up onto the insanely tall bed and sit at the edge ignoring his raised eyebrow. But now at seventeen she simply told him what she was going to do.

She nearly tripped with cake in hand, when she walked in to see him stripping the linens in just a pair of pajama pants. Her eyes made sure to quickly take everything in, shirtless Mikhail was a rare treat for her. The man hardly changed since the first time she met him, he stood six foot five, still shaved his head, the icy blue eyes only seemed to get more piercing somehow. But she did notice his body changed in size, his broad shoulders seemed stronger while his chest seemed thicker. The rock hard abs covered in tattoos rippled nicely as he expertly flicked the cover into place.

"Did you just come in to stare at me?" his glacial gaze swept over her making her wish she worn something nicer beside worn faded jeans and an old oversized flannel shirt.

Ignoring his remark she proceeded as planned. "Happy birthday!" Carefully she sat the cake down on the nightstand by her and vaulted onto the fresh sheets before grabbing the cake again. Patiently she waited for him to sit back down against the pillows.

"I got you that cake you like so much." his growling grunt of approval, as he forked into the cake, made her smile even more. No one who wasn't close to him would suspect it, but Mikhail loved sweets. Boldly she leaned onto the massive naked shoulder and forked the chocolate cake taking a small bite.
Realizing she could lay like this forever, she hurriedly handed him the tiny shiny blue box. From her position, he watched his hand deftly open the package letting the balloons fly to the ceiling.

"You made me a CD," turning the CD over he read the back. Twelve intricate violin solos constructed with the most care.

"Yeah I have been working on it for a while now."

"I don't want you wasting your..."

"Mikhail! Don't say that right after I give it to you!" she exclaimed loudly sitting up now with her hands on her hips, "Besides, I haven't wasted anything, I did it because I love you and it's your b-day," she could see the glacial eyes turn dark, it unnerved him when she confessed her love. But she always ignored him and kept on doing it, maybe one day he would say it back. Pushing away the pang of disappointment in her chest she pressed on.

"Besides you only turn twenty-eight once in a lifetime." laughing at his groan over the mention of his age she snuggled back into his hard shoulder.

Misha held her breath as he removed the rest of the wrapping to see two familiar handmade slips fall to his lap. Daring not to look at his face Misha remained deathly still as he grabbed the pieces of paper.

"I see that I got my customary coupons." His deep accented voice held a touch of humor.

Her mind told her she should have been relieved he found it humorous, but the pain that jolted through her heart persisted. Misha wasn't sure when it started, but her feelings for Mikhail had turned from hero worship to something more. The love she had for him turned into an ache. Pathetic as it may be, the only thing that ever quelled the dull ache was receiving any sort of attention from the man.

Unlike Krill, Mikhail did not say or show his affection for her. There were no kisses on the cheek, or great big bear hugs like Krill gave her, just stoic looks and occasional smirks. For nearly four years now she had been giving Mikhail "affection coupons," she wouldn't dare call them "love" coupons as she has seen them referenced online. They were just small things, such as one free hug or one free kiss. And every time Mikhail had the same response: leaning over he put the coupons in the second drawer of his nightstand. Which by now was most likely full of unused coupons.

Giving off a small sigh she sat up and crossed her legs. "So what do you want to do for your birthday?"

Of course, she already knew the answer to her question. Work. Just as he did every day, he was going to run off to his precious shipyards and make Vladimir more money. Hoping her disappointment didn't show, she fiddled with the torn wrapping as she waited for the customary response.

"I want you to go get your violin and play me one of the songs on this CD."

Mikhail watched her face light up in elation, for some reason he could never get tired of her large smile. Somehow the little street urchin he decided to shelter had become this radiant talented woman beneath his roof. Though technically he was present through her progression from childhood to adulthood, Mikhail never really saw it that way. Krill was left in charge of raising her, to Mikhail he simply viewed her as a roommate.

Their morning talks started off as mini Russian lessons and transformed into random talks about everything under the sun. Misha was unlike anyone he ever met. She was bold, strong, stubborn, smart and caring. There was no fear when she looked him in the eyes, no favors she wanted, and not to mention she expressed her love to him daily. Never before had he felt such a complete overwhelming emotion. Frankly he still couldn't figure out how to react to it though he expressed his dissatisfaction to her routine declarations, he did nothing to outright stop them.

Watching her hop from his bed, he could hear her feet pound the floor as she ran to the other side of the condo to retrieve her violin. Back within seconds she scrambled back onto his bed and knelt into the fluffy comforter and took her position.

Slowly the urchin turned prodigy, filled the air with dark full tones of sadness. Watching her play was one of the rare times he could observe her without notice. Instead of her usual long braid, Misha's trademark puffy black curls were let loose this morning. The long black curls were pushed to the side of her bent head giving her plenty of undisturbed room as she drew her bow back and forth.

This position allowed him to see her complete profile. As far as her face was concerned, Misha had not changed much from the first day they meet. The large eyes that intrigued him remained the bright focal point to her face, the large brown eyes were surrounded by long dark curly lashes. Not that he didn't expect Misha to grow into a fine young woman, Mikhail just wasn't prepared for the level of beauty. Of course, she was a bit taller from when she initially moved in though she only stood chest height causing her to have to look up at him, especially when she was angry, which was his favorite. The flashes of annoyance that would sizzle through her gaze when she tried to calmly state her case never got old. Which in turn led him to purposely crowd her even more.

Sitting against the tall headboard with one leg pulled up Mikhail listened to that sad notes that blanketed the air. Misha's specialty not only lay in her masterful skill with the instrument, but it resided in her ability to send the listener on a roller coaster ride of sadness. The song began slow and melancholic then turned to deep tones of loss leaving the listener completely encased in their emotions, it wasn't until the very end would she sprinkle in one or two brighter notes.

No one could figure out why she preferred such doleful pieces, but Mikhail had a theory. He figured it might have had something to do with the fact that Misha never cried. Every day she remained bright and sunny no matter the circumstances, nor the memories of her painful past. Mikhail could only recall one gut wrenching moment where he saw tears fall from her large beautiful eyes.

~*~*~

A couple of weeks passed since the moment Mikhail was forced to remind his crew exactly what he was about at Abram's garage. A wired jaw and thirty-four stitches later an example was successfully made that day. Frustration however, seemed to find him all over again due to one simple question from Misha's new legal guardian.

They were sitting at their usual table in the backroom at The Rose one night, Abram was at the bar flirting with a waitress and Krill was sitting to Mikhail's right. They were talking about the opening of Krill's new night club Vital when the question came out of nowhere. In the most casual way, Krill asked about Misha moving in with him.

Mikhail could vividly recall the feeling that went through him when the Krill asked him, hell the gut punching feeling went through him every time he replayed the question. Mikhail should have seen this coming. For starters Mikhail spoiled his captains, they got everything they wanted from him. Any business scheme they offered, Mikhail approved. Any favor needed Mikhail granted. Mikhail couldn't really discern if he was just fortunate to have really smart captains or he was just a pushover and never realized it.

Secondly Krill had a father complex. It was one of the main reasons he let Krill get so close to Misha. Krill had a daughter who disowned him back in Russia due to Krill's choice in profession. Since she never wanted anything to do with him, Krill never got to see her again or the grandchild he never got to meet. Giving him guardianship to Misha not only solved Mikhail's problem on how to take care of the kid, but it strengthened Krill's loyalty to him tenfold. The man was beyond happy. Thankfully Abram's boisterous return to the table sparked up another topic leaving Mikhail time to mull over the question.

By the next morning, the question was still burning a hole through him. Krill would be the best option for the kid, not to mention it would solve any sort of gossiping problems that dare to spring up again. But every other part of Mikhail passionately rebuked the notion of her leaving. He had gotten used to her, he enjoyed their morning talks, he rather liked her ramblings about the music program after school. Since he never really watched TV, Mikhail looked at her as sort of an entertainment source.

The frustration only consumed him more when he walked into the kitchen that morning to see the bright eyed kid eagerly waiting for him at the kitchen counter.

Swiping his keys from the nearby table, he looked at her, "I don't have time for breakfast."

Not missing the disappointment in her eyes Mikhail quickly stepped out of the door and onto the elevator. Handing his briefcase to Nico in the lobby, Mikhail passed the concierge desk ignoring the vapid red head trying to get his attention.

With a quick command to drive Mikhail deviated from his customary routine. Normally he would come down the elevator with

Misha and watch her walk to the school bus-stop, down the street. Stamping down the pang of guilt, he focused on the upcoming day's work.

Stuffing her lunch into her bag Misha slowly put on her red coat that Krill bought. She wondered what she did to make Mikhail look so angry at her this morning. When she went to bed last night, he wasn't home yet so it couldn't have been that. Maybe it was something from "work," sometimes he came home with bloody shirts or talking really fast in Russian on the phone to one of his enforcers. Doing her best to think positive she grabbed the matching hat and went down the elevator. Since she didn't have a key to the place she went to the concierge desk.

"Excuse me." The tall red haired lady was quite beautiful, she reminded her of some of the women that Mikhail brought over to his room some nights. She was really tall and thin, she even wore the same expression like all the other women. It was as if they were looking down their nose at everything unless it was Mikhail. When they saw Mikhail, each and every one of them turned into a different person, they blinked a lot and permanently wore a smile.

"Yes." Her tone was as if she was being bothered.

"I was wondering if you could lock Mikhail Kulakov's unit for me," she gave the woman her brightest smile. "Since I don't have a key."

A strange look crossed the woman's face before nodding. Not wanting to be late Misha thanked her quickly, pulling the straps of her purple Hello Kitty backpack tighter on her back she ran to the bus stop.

At school she forgot about Mikhail's unusual mood, Misha found school simply amazing, the teachers were nice, she got to eat a second breakfast and even lunch because Krill bought her the meal plan, and she even made friends. But the best part was the music program, every day for an hour she got to learn and play the violin after school. Every since she read a mystery novel at the library, where the detective solved a crime at the symphony, she wanted to play the violin.

By the time the bus dropped her off at her stop there were only a few rays of sunlight left. Though it stopped snowing it was still really cold out. The wind whipped around her as she walked down the street to Mikhail's shiny blue building. Reaching for the heavy glass door, she pulled it open allowing her to step into the warm lobby. Walking to the concierge desk, she smiled at the same red haired lady.

"Hi again," she chirped loudly over the tall reception desk. "I was wondering if you could let me into Mikhail's unit."

For a moment there the lady didn't answer, she just stared at her with great concentration, after a couple of seconds she came from around her desk smiling softly.

"I am so sorry, but I was told to tell you that Mikhail no longer wants you around."

Silence. Misha had to repeat what she said a couple of times in her head. A numbing feeling spread from her fingers to her toes. This couldn't be happening. That couldn't be right. "I don't under..." Misha's words seemed to have gotten stuck in her throat.

"All your things were thrown into the dumpster out back." by now the red haired was not so gently guiding her back through the front doors. Misha felt as if her heart was going to explode, she couldn't respond she could barely even process what was happening. The biting cold wind in her face allowed her to focus on her surroundings again, looking up she saw the red haired lady look at her with emotionless eyes.

"I am sorry, but you will have to go." and with that she shut the door, leaving Misha out in the cold.

As if in a trance Misha shifted the purple kitty backpack on her back as she walked around the building. With her eyes wide she stopped in her tracks as she stared at the familiar bed frame and small white dresser leaning against the dumpsters.

She should have said something to him this morning. She should have done something. Anything, she would have done or said anything if she only would have known what she did wrong.

After receiving the frantic phone call from Krill, Mikhail broke every traffic law to make it to his place. Slamming the car in park out front, Mikhail walked into the lobby to see Abram and Nico standing around the pacing Krill.

"She isn't here Mikhail!" Krill's voice boomed throughout the lobby. "I came by to unlock the door for her after you called to tell me you left early this morning. I got here a little after her music class would have let out, and she wasn't here. I had Nico check the school, and she wasn't there, they said she got on the bus. Abram tracked down the bus driver and the bus driver said he dropped her off at the stop. And she says," He was pointing to the frightened looking red head concierge, "she hasn't seen Misha either." at this point Krill was all but yelling.

Ignoring the clenching feeling in his gut Mikhail tried to stay calm and think this through. The last time he saw Misha he left her at the kitchen counter, the look of her disappointment stayed with him all day. But that wouldn't have made her run off. Would it?

"Ok Krill you stay here in case she turns up, Abram, Nico you two come with me." Walking to his car with the two in tow, he quickly gave orders for where they should look. Jumping into his car, Mikhail decided to retrace the bus route himself. A part of him couldn't believe he was going to go out searching for this kid, but he had a gut feeling that something was wrong. The last time he ignored his gut when it came to Misha she almost got molested and possibly killed.

Gripping the steering wheel tighter, he made his way down the dark streets. With every mile passed the sense of urgency grew stronger. After retracing the entire route Mikhail turned the corner that led back to his building, he glanced at the bus stop. The tiny red dot made Mikhail slam on his breaks. Getting out of the car Mikhail stalked up to the dimly lit bus stop and stopped. Holding her backpack in her lap, Misha hugged the bag close as she held her head face down in the purple plastic bag. He couldn't see her face, but he knew from a glance it was her.

"What in the hell do you think you're doing?!" he roared causing her to jolt upright. The normally bright eyes were swollen and red as they stared at him in shock.

"Mikhail." his name was barely a whisper. The anger that flared in him seeing her sitting at the bus stop disappeared as she stared at him as if he were a ghost. "You came back."

"Misha what in the hell are you talking about?" Not waiting for her to answer he picked up her bag with one hand and hoisted her off the cold bench in the other arm. Silently he stuffed her into the front seat and drove quickly into the condo garage. Taking the private elevator directly up to his unit, they were greeted by Krill's booming voice.

"Misha!" without warning the larger man snatched her into his arms. Stepping past them, Mikhail dropped the purple bag on the couch and grabbed a drink. He was disgusted with himself that he let this kid manipulate him into dropping everything he was doing and call for a search for her, only to find the little cur was trying to leave him. Swallowing the vodka, he slammed down the glass.

"Krill put her down," Slowly Krill put her down. Misha still looking at him as if she was looking at a ghost, walked over to where he was standing. "What in the fuck did..."

"I'll do anything." the alarming words cut off his inquisition. Furrowing his brow Mikhail looked to Krill for answers only to see him looking just as confused.

"Misha what the hell are you talking about?"

"I'll do anything. Anything. I'll sleep on the floor. I'll even sleep on

the balcony, please just don't be mad at me. Please don't make me go," by now her voice was warbling in distress. Tears started to roll down her eyes, eyes that were filled with wild desperation. Her hands were outstretched as she stepped
   closer and closer to him. "I promise I will be good, whatever I did please just..."

"Misha stop it!" by now she was grabbing his pants. The harsh command startled her, bringing even more tears down her face. Holding up his hand he stopped Krill from coming closer, the man looked as if he was dying watching her cry. Sitting down to get closer to eye level with her Mikhail grabbed her by the shoulders. "Misha tell me what is going on? Why did you leave? What are you talking about?" Mikhail did his best to keep his voice calm.

"She said you kicked me out and you threw away my things." her words sent a chill through each man.

Doing his best to remain calm, Mikhail asked the question for verification. "Who said this?"

"The red haired lady downstairs, she said..." Ignoring her repeat the vile lies, Mikhail looked over her head to Krill. Thankfully Misha wasn't facing Krill at the moment, the child loved him like a father, she shouldn't see the look of an enraged killer on the face she came to love. Without anything being said Krill walked out the front door without a sound. Looking back to Misha, Mikhail tuned back into what she was saying. "I promise Mikhail I promise to be good please, I don't need anything..."

Sickened by the turn of events Mikhail grabbed her hand and pulled her down the hallway. Shoving her room door open he pulled her into the room.

"I had all your furniture replaced today, that is why your old stuff was by the dumpster," Looking around the room he damn near spit in disgust. He bought and ordered this stuff this morning at work while being haunted with her sad face from that morning. Truth be told he was kind of looking forward to seeing her reaction. But now it was completely ruined due to that foul disgusting bitch.

After taking nearly a half an hour reassuring her that he had no intention to kick her out, Mikhail finally got her to let go of him and go to sleep. Just thinking of her uncertain tear filled eyes as he shut her door filled him with a dark anger. Earlier while he was waiting for her to get cleaned up, he spoke to Krill on the phone. Krill told him that he called Vera in to deal with Christina, the red haired concierge. Supposedly the woman thought that Misha was standing in the way of some sort of fictional relationship she made up for Mikhail. Knowing Vera she was most likely going disfigure the woman's face...first. Ordering Krill to make sure Vera did not kill the bitch, Mikhail didn't need the extra work of a dead body. He tossed his phone on the couch beside him and leaned his head back against the cushions.

From the moment he met her, Mikhail actually felt something for the first time in years. The ennui that shadowed him seemed to dissipate once she stepped into his life. However, Mikhail could safely say he didn't factor in the other emotions she would create. Misha's desperate pleas rang in his head. 'I will be good.' Mikhail nearly laughed in disgust. Hell Misha couldn't get any better if she tried. She was an angel surrounded by devils.

Seeing her tiny form huddled on the bus stop, hearing her desperate pleas, or even her reluctance for him to leave her side when she prepared for bed all brought him to a rage. It was never his intention to keep the kid, he honestly didn't know what he wanted her around for, so when he found himself declining Krill's request and ordering white and purple bedroom furniture it was rather surprising. Mikhail could only wonder what other changes Misha would bring to his life.

Since that day, Mikhail made it a priority to keep the radiant smile on her face. Misha was unlike anyone he ever met, definitely unlike any other women he met, she didn't require much to keep her happy, books were her entertainment and music was her passion.

Playing the final cord Misha put the bow down, pulling her legs from her kneeling position she sat in the middle of the large bed. Looking up at him she met the intense blue gaze directly. She was thankful he could not see the goosebumps that ran through her due to her long sleeves. It was these rare moments of silence she felt that when he looked at her, he could see right through her. Misha knew Mikhail was well versed in reading people, quickly accessing what kind of person they were, and he was particularly adept at reading her.

For as along as she known him, she was never able to hide anything from him whether it be surprises, sickness, worries, nothing escaped his notice. Well almost nothing. Thankfully he never noticed her growing feelings. Just the thought of his disproving look made he want to crawl away and die. Putting on her biggest smile, she pushed all her thoughts of him out of her mind just in case.

"Your song was beautiful."

"Well technically it's your song I wrote it just for you." daring to scoot closer, she settled carefully against the pillows next to him. "I won't even be performing any of those songs at the concerto next week. These are all for you."

Feeling the bed dip slightly from his weight shifting as he got up from the bed he looked at her, "Thank you again." The faint smile would have made her night if it wasn't accompanied by him giving her the familiar dismissal look. She has seen that look dozens of times before, times when he and his captains were about to discuss business or when she was at his office and he needed to work.

Scooting off the bed she grabbed her instrument and walked towards his door. Boldly she turned around, "Are you going out to one of Krill's clubs?" the moment the question was out of her mouth she wished she just would have walked out the door initially.

The question was pretty much an accusation that he was going to pick up another woman. Like watching a train wreck she watched him slowly lift one eyebrow in response to her audacious question.

Not sticking around to dig herself deeper into embarrassment she quickly walked down the hallway across the condo into her room.

Shutting her door she let out a ragged sigh. Why would she say that? It was as if the disappointment of being dismissed externalized itself into a bratty question that just popped out of her mouth. How could she be so stupid? Trying not to think about the embarrassing scene she buried herself in her sheet music for the rest of the night.

Chapter 6

Leaning against the wall in his elevator, Mikhail let his mind wander to his birthday events the previous week. Indeed after spending the morning with Misha he did go to one of his nightclubs Krill managed. Mikhail couldn't get over Misha's unusual behavior that day. Never did she question his dating habits, it was so out of place he honestly wasn't sure how to respond.

Since then she has been avoiding him, the past couple of mornings consisted of brief goodbyes as she rushed out of the door as he was coming from his room. It was ludicrous because they were going to the same damn place. When she graduated high school early, he gave her the empty storehouse next to his office in the shipyards for a sound studio. The building was more or less a small storage unit he pondered destroying once, but when he overheard her talking to her friends about possibly renting a studio space, Mikhail found a way to kill two birds with one stone.

Just remembering her shocked reaction to his gift brought him a sense of satisfaction. Mikhail reveled in eliciting new emotions and expressions from Misha. In a way, he kind of likened her to a puppy at times. He secretly loved her responses to his attentions, and when he was done, he could simply leave for her to entertain herself. However, this new pattern of her avoiding him was starting to irritate him.

Stepping off the elevator, he stepped into the living area and paused. The sounds of grunts and whimpering came from down Misha's hallway. Immediately every nerve his body was on fire. A killing rage he hadn't felt since his days in Russia overtook his body. The sheer thought of some man in her room causing these sounds darkened his vision with red. Stalking to her room with silent, lethal grace, Mikhail slammed the door open to her room.

Standing in the middle of the room was Misha—shirtless.

For the longest of moments, he simply stared at her frozen form. Mikhail quickly gathered he must have interrupted her trying to put on the long gold formal gown she had halfway up. Since she was standing to the side, he was allowed not only to see her slender naked torso, but the sides of her uncovered breast peeked out from the gown she was holding in place.

"Mikhail." her shocked whisper brought them both back to reality. Averting his eyes from her partially covered breast, he looked into her shocked brown eyes.

He should be apologizing and or at least stepping back, giving her privacy, but instead he found himself stepping into her room even more. "What are you doing?"

Misha was sure her heart was going to just stop beating then and there. The flash of pure rage on his face as he burst into her room scared her more than his entrance. But it was his darkening gaze on her that made her heart constrict. Under his deep gaze she forgot how to move, it wasn't until his baritone question filtered into the air did she remember her state of undress.

Clutching the sequined material closer Misha turned her back slightly to Mikhail, praying her loose hair would hide most of her naked back.

"I was trying to put on this dress, you know for the performance" God why did her voice have to sound so shaky, "and I was having a hard time zipping it up." Not to mention getting it over her hips.

Not being able to see him from her new position, Misha started to turn her head to look over her shoulder when there was no response. The warm hands on her naked waist nearly caused her to cry out, but thankfully she bit her lips to stop herself.

"Here let me," the deep voice was close to her ear now, "hold this." Briefly the warm pad of his fingers swept across the back of her bare shoulders, as he gathered her hair bringing it around over her shoulder. Nervously she let go of the front of the dress, thanking

God the fabric was stiff enough to somewhat stay in place over her breast as she grabbed her gathered hair.

Now more than ever she felt the silence in the room. While the length of her naked back was exposed to him, she focused on the movements of his large hands. Gently he pulled the dress together at the top and hooked it together. Misha felt faint as his hands slid down the curve of her hips to reach the bottom of the zipper. Biting her lips she focused intently on the pressure his hands made at the top of her butt. With one firm grip around her waist and the other on the zipper he slowly pulled it up. The sound of the zipper echoed loudly through the room as it slowly ascend up the gold dress.

"Done." Before she could dwell on why a flash of disappointment hit her with his remark, she felt his hands grip her waist and quickly turn her, causing her to reach out for his shoulders for support at the quick movement.

"Mik--,"

"You look beautiful." his deep accented words effectively cut off whatever she was going to say. Though she had her footing by now she dared not move a muscle, she just looked up at the man staring down at her.

The distant sound of Mikhail's cellphone ringing broke the moment. Stepping back Mikhail turned and left her room, leaving her to stand dumbfounded in the same spot. Letting out a long breath she didn't realize she was holding, she leaned against the bed. Looking at herself in the mirror across the room, Misha smiled, the dress fit her perfectly just like Letisha, her best friend, said it would. But even if the dress didn't fit she would keep it just so she could have a permanent reminder of this moment.

For what seemed like forever Misha had been wanting any sort of contact from the man. Mikhail never received hugs, never received kisses, and he definitely never initiated contact of any sort. Though she tried not to, Misha's whole body tingled slightly just recalling the feeling of his hands. She kept telling herself that her growing feelings for the stoic man were wrong. Mikhail Kulakov did not look at her in that way nor would he ever. It would be selfish of her to try to change the tide of their friendship—no matter how much she wanted to.

Now how the hell was she going to get out of the dress?

He was a pedophile. His men were right. He was a pedophile.

His thoughts were running away with him at this point. Locking the sliding door to his hallway, Mikhail stomped into his room and let out a frustrated sigh. Angrily he stripped out of his slacks and crisp white button down and threw them onto the floor. Changing into his workout clothes he went across the hall to his private gym.

My God he should have turned around once he saw that there was no man in her room, especially when he saw that she was just trying to get dressed. But the moment he saw the smooth brown skin he was trapped.

Lifting the dumbbell, Mikhail clenched his eyes shut in disgust as he replayed the scene in his head. When she turned her back to him, Mikhail realized she was completely naked under that dress, the slight peak of her perfectly round ass from the gaping zipper sealed his fate. Mikhail couldn't stop himself from touching her, he couldn't stop himself from basking in her feminine apprehension. The blood in his body rushed even now as he recalled his hands gliding over the flare of her hips.

Never before did he notice what a woman Misha grew into. From her odd sense of style of wearing baggy clothing and him viewing her pretty much a kid, Mikhail never had a chance to notice. Changing to the punching bag, Mikhail nearly laughed in self disgust when he thought of his earlier references to Misha. Gone were the thoughts of her just being the puppy-like kid that followed him around, now the image of her brown eyes looking at him with shock while she covered her naked breast was all he could conjure.

And that's why he was a pedophile. A sick bastard that would feel up a young woman while getting dressed, a young woman who trusted him implacably. A trust he no longer deserved. Punching the bag with an almighty force, Mikhail remembered the dark feeling that washed over him when he heard the sounds from the living room. Just as he never thought of her as a woman, nor did the thought of Misha dating ever cross his mind.

Well, actually it did once.

A couple of years ago while Misha was still in high school, he came home early, only to find a large boy sitting in his living room snuggled up to Misha on his couch. Again his brain seemed to revert to his days in Russia. Kill first, ask questions later. Thankfully Misha caught his presence before he could act. She quickly introduced the insanely tall kid to him as Jay, one of the friends she always talked about. Jay was a good looking black guy, he was as tall as Mikhail, had an easy going personality, and always showed respect. A calm swept over him when Mikhail remembered her previous ramblings about the kid. From his recollection, Jay played drums at the art school both he and Misha attended, was a talented vocalist, and more importantly Jay liked men.

Therefore, Jay lived to see another day.

But since then Mikhail was never given another reason to be concerned about Misha dating. She was completely engrossed in her musical career. When her friends got together, all they did was make music and or talk about music.

If he weren't such a sick bastard, the thought of Misha finding a nice guy and getting married wouldn't make him want to kill something. God, but the thought of some man on top of her and touching her made him want to vomit. Sighing raggedly he took a swig of water from his bottle. Pushing the thoughts of Misha's future out of his mind, he would save those for another time, when he would be better equipped to handle them.

But how could things ever be the same now? Would Misha look at him with fear or disgust? Just the thought of her not wanting to be around him filled him with renewed discipline.

Dripping with sweat, he leaned against the matted wall and made a decision. He was going to push the memory of today's events deep into his mind. He was going to lock it away with all the other dark memories. Misha meant more to him than anything in this world. Tomorrow was a new day, and he was going to pretend as if this day never happened.

Chapter 7

Today was the day of her concerto at the Symphony Hall, her and five other young and upcoming musicians will be playing solos for over two thousand guests. Though tonight was an important night for her, all she could think about was the scene between her and Mikhail earlier that week.

Misha told herself to forget about it, that it would do nobody any good thinking about it. But the more she tried to rebuke it the more she thought about him. The thoughts even crept in at night. Feeling herself flush with embarrassment Misha sat on the rim of her tub with her head in her hands as she thought of what she did last night.

Partly nervous and partly frustrated Misha had a tough time sleeping before any event. Silently she moved her fingers on the imaginative violin as she lay in bed thinking about the difficult parts of the piece she was going to play. The frustration, however, was caused my Mikhail, just as he did for every event in the past he wished her well the night before, meaning he wasn't going to attend as per usual. Vera told her long ago it was because of her safety that Mikhail did not attend. It was already common knowledge that he harbored a young kid in his home, but he didn't want to bring any further attention to it in case he gained bold enemies.

But Misha didn't believe that, she just thought Mikhail simply didn't want to go. Mikhail never did anything he didn't want to do. Why should he be bothered with her performances? Though the thought of his attendance never bothered her before the performance, it was only when it came to the day of the event that she felt the stinging hurt. Though she reminded herself every time, she should be grateful, it was Mikhail who purchased her expensive violins, and it was Mikhail she owed everything.

Tossing and turning her thoughts jumped from her frustration with Mikhail to other frustrations Mikhail caused her. She recalled the feeling of his rough hands on her waist that day, bringing the tingling feeling back again. In the sanctity of her bed, lit with only the moon's light from the wall of windows she let her hand slide under her sheets. Slowly she glided her fingers across the crisp curls, closing her eyes she imagined what would have happened if his phone never rang.

What would have happened if he stayed? Would he have unzipped her dress and kissed her breast? By now she could feel the dampness between her legs. Or would he have simply lifted up the long gown to discover she wasn't wearing any underwear? Letting her thoughts run wild, reenacting all the scenes from novels she read before, she brought on her breathy climax that in turn brought on shame the next morning.

Standing up from the rim of the tub, she quickly stuffed her things into her performance bag doing her best to forget what happened. She should just take a page from Mikhail's book, she thought in slight annoyance, the man acted as if nothing happened. He even woke up early to force her to keep to their morning breakfast routine, which she had even more of a reason to duck out of. Though she was peeved he could act with such aplomb after their situation, she was admittedly happy that nothing changed for the worse. It would have killed her if she lost him due to her childish crush.

Grabbing her violin case, her bag, and dress bag she rode the elevator down to the lobby. Standing there waiting for her was Leo Maslak, her designated guard. Every since she graduated Krill felt it necessary that she have an escort for her safety. Since she didn't drive Misha was completely OK with not taking the bus, besides her an Leo got along just fine. Standing a little taller than her in his black slacks and dress shirt Leo was the typical bad boy image that girls swooned over, and he knew it too. Leo made sure his blonde hair was perfectly styled to portray just a touch of disheveled care, his shirt was purposely rolled up to reveal all his tattoos he was so proud of, all the while wearing his signature devilish smirk.

"Here let me have these," grabbing her dress he carefully slung it over one shoulder while throwing the purple duffel bag over the other. Misha trusted no one with her violin, she carried that herself.

"You nervous?" he asked as he opened the passenger door for her.

"Yeah," she replied. After putting her things away, he settled into the driver's seat of the black Volvo and pulled off.

"Well don't be, you're the best violinist, there is no reason for a pro like yourself to be nervous." his confidence for her made her smile, Leo was always sweet to her.

"Well, I don't know about the best. But thank you anyways you're my best motivator."

If Leo could help it, he would be Misha's only motivator. From the moment he met Misha, Leo's life changed, she made him want to be a better man. There was no one sweeter or kinder than Misha. For Misha unlike most forgiveness came easily, though he deserved her forgiveness the least. Everyone loved Misha, much to Leo's annoyance, every soldier under Mikhail's command who had the privilege of meeting Misha was instantly entranced.

On the rare occasions she would come up to the Rose with Krill she would have the whole backroom at her beck and call if she wanted. But Misha wasn't the type of woman that would hungrily seek attention, she simply didn't need to. Ever smiling she would talk to the people she knew as if they were long time pals forcing the people that didn't know her to want to make her acquaintance.

For brief moments, they got to enjoy her beacon of innocence when she visited the Rose until Mikhail came in-- stealing her spotlight. Whenever Mikhail entered the room she would disengage from any conversation, quickly fold from any poker game she was attempting to win, and quickly magnetize to his side. Leo would watch furtively from his table as the boss waited expectantly for her to come running to his side. Leo would do anything for Misha to look at him the way she looked at the boss. He more than enjoyed his duty as her guard, he worked hard to gain back trust to get to this position.

Parking the car, Leo grabbed her things and followed her into the symphony, after finding her dressing room he followed her to rehearsal. Grabbing a stool, he watched her practice in the empty hall, watched her talk to the light technicians and work with the sound crew for her requirements. Unlike other women, Misha wasn't so easy to win over, Leo liked that the most. Just as she practiced every day at her craft so did Leo.

He was determined to make Misha see him.

If it wasn't for Vera, Misha wasn't sure how she could manage most things in her life. Every since the day Misha meet Vera they were close. Misha looked at her as the mother she should have had. Currently, She was helping Misha get into the gold sequined gown.

"Mmm we are going to need some tape for your boobs." turning around she began scrounging in her Louis Vuitton bag she always carried. Vera was a sucker for fashion, unlike herself Vera never left her house without a carefully put together assemble. Tonight she was wearing a short black cocktail dress that accentuated her slender frame perfectly.

"Oh, well I kinda thought the built in bra on the dress would be enough," Misha mumbled looking warily at the strip of body tape Vera was applying.

"Ha! With boobs and ass like yours sweetheart you can never just blindly trust the outfit," she laughed as she pulled another piece of tape. "You could be up there in the middle of your song that requires the most movement and BAM—out goes your boob." Vera must have noticed how still Misha got, looking up to her shocked face Vera laughed again. "But you won't have to worry about that sweety, even though this gown is strapless I am going to tape you up so good its going to take me, Letisha, and Jay to pry you out."

Misha let out a sigh of relief at the woman's assurance. If anyone knew about this kind of thing, it would be Vera. The ex-stripper was now the manager of two high-end strip clubs Krill owned. Vera oversaw every aspect to the dancers, the human resources end, and even the outfits.

"Is Letisha and Jay here yet?" Misha looked up through the mirror as Vera was putting the final touches on her newly straightened hair. Normally Misha wore her hair curly, so on the few occasions she did wear it straight it felt very odd.

"Yes, there sitting next to me and Krill." smoothing out her dress one final time Vera stepped back and looked at her. "There your done."

Turning around Misha looked in the large mirror, her reflection made her smile. With her long straight hair that slightly grazed her waist, she stood tall in the gold matching heels to her strapless gown. The weight of the material made her feel as if she were wearing sparkly armor. Turning around she caught the moisture in Vera's eyes, walking forward she quickly hugged the older woman.

"I love you, Vera. Thank you again for everything."

Wordlessly Vera nodded and pulled away just as they hear a knock on her door.

"Its time Ms. Abosi." the urgent voice of the stage director signaled her time to go.

Gathering her instrument Misha walked out of the dressing room and followed the young man. As she followed the stage director to her spot, she caught sight of Leo amongst the backstage bustle of people. Smiling she quickly waved at her guard before catching up to where she was supposed to go.

Standing at the side of the stage well out of sight of the audience, she took a deep breath as she absently watched the cellist finish up on stage. Taking her cue, she lifted her head high and walked in front of the bright lights.

After a long internal debate, Mikhail found himself sitting in the crowded symphony watching a rather boring cello performance. Moments before Vera quietly snuck in to sit in the empty seat between him an Letisha. Next to the smiling Letisha was an equally happy Jay, both were excited for the next performance. Excitement was an understatement when it came to the man sitting next to him. Mikhail nearly rolled his eyes at Krill's fidgeting, the man looked as if he either wanted to cry or shout for joy. Vera on the other hand was covertly dabbing away the moisture in her eyes with her designer handkerchief.

Though he didn't look it, Mikhail was slightly nervous. After debating for nearly an hour, he arrived late, missing the first two performances. Thankfully Misha's performance was saved until the end, they saved the strongest player for last, or at least that was what Krill chirped happily about as he made room for him to sit. The surprise on everyone's face at his sudden attendance was annoying.

"Misha will be so happy that you are here." Krill's voice silenced abruptly as the clapping died down.

The shimmer of a familiar gold dress completely silenced the audience as the violinist took the stage. Though he has known the performer most of her life, Mikhail felt as if this was the first time he saw her in such a light. With her long black hair bone straight and the skin tight gold dress, Misha stood there sparkling beautifully under the stage lights.

Slowly she positioned her instrument and raised her bow.

The song was like anything he ever heard from her before. It was the most detailed piece he has ever heard her play, all the while she remained still like a golden statue with her eyes closed as her arms worked in a frenzy to produce the stirring sounds. By the time the piece was over, he felt as if his heart were beating ten times faster. There was a moment of silence, just enough time for her to let down her bow, before everyone in the audience stood with a roar of applause.

Even from his position her could see her flush slightly in embarrassment. Making a quick bow as she picked up some of the thrown flowers she rushed off the stage.

Through all of the pats on the back and congratulations Misha had a hard time catching her breath, thankfully Leo appeared out of nowhere to escort her to her dressing room. She needed to freshen up before she attended the reception.

"You were wonderful," Leo whispered in her ear as he guided her through the packed backstage.

Still a bundle of nerves Misha didn't trust herself to speak, she simply squeezed his hand in acknowledgment.

Ushering her into the dressing room Leo stood in the doorway smiling gently, "I will wait out here."

Nodding she closed the door, letting out a loud sigh. She couldn't believe it. She did it. That impossible piece her tutor warned her against she completed it flawlessly. Misha wanted to cry in happiness, but she feared she would ruin the makeup Vera painstakingly applied though knowing Vera it was probably typhoon proof.

Leaning against her dresser, she heard the hard knock at her door, thinking it was Leo she opened the door.

Standing on the other side carrying a large bouquet of dark purple roses was Mikhail. Stepping forward he partially closed the door behind him. Misha couldn't move or say anything, she was so shocked.

"I wanted to give you these before your reception," His deep voice washed over as he stood inches away. Though Mikhail dressed up every day, Misha never seen him look this good. He wore a dark blue suit that was perfectly tailored to his tall, lithe form. Misha's gaze expertly noticed how his broad shoulders filled out the jacket as well as the bulge of his biceps through the dark material. Unlike his scruffy look, last night his head was freshly shaven for the event.

"You came," she half squeaked half whispered. "Did you see the performance?"

He graced her with a rare smile as she carefully took the roses. "Yes, I did. You were magnificent."

Smiling she clutched the roses tighter, "Thank you so much, Mikhail. You don't know how much I wanted you to see it." at this point she really did feel the stinging pain of tears in her eyes, doing her best to hold them back she smiled brighter.

"I also wanted to redeem this before your reception."

Looking down she watched in stunned silence as he pulled a familiar pink slip of paper from his pocket. It was one of the kiss coupons. Taking the paper, she carefully looked up to meet his unnerving gaze. The feeling of his warm, callused hand on her chin shocked her allowing him to easily tilt her head to his liking. All too quickly he leaned down and brushed his lips across hers.

Though someone looking in probably wouldn't have considered it a real kiss Misha, however, felt as if her whole body was on fire. She could only thank God she was somewhat leaning against the vanity or she would have made a fool out of herself.

In a daze, she watched one of his rare smiles form at her obvious shock.

"I will see you after the reception." Misha just stood there frozen in the same spot as the door closed. My God she couldn't believe it. She actually got a kiss from Mikhail. The thought of him bringing her the coupon just for that, made her dizzy with excitement.

The familiar chime of a text message broke her out of her thoughts, looking at her phone she quickly read the impatient text from her agent. He was waiting for her so that they could begin their mingle. For an artist this was the most important time after a performance, this is where valuable connections were made. Any other time Misha would have been excited to attend, but now all she wanted to do was run back to Mikhail's side. Forgoing on changing into the gray cocktail dress she bought Misha quickly freshened up and walked out to the waiting Leo.

Walking with the silent Leo down to the reception area, she thought about Mikhail. She wondered if he brought any more coupons because Misha was not against snatching some nearby paper and scribbling some down.

Watching absently from the doorway to the reception area Leo stared through the throng of people at the shimmering beauty. Still dressed in her performance dress she dazzled as she mingled with fans. Leo's eyes narrowed as he recalled the scene in her dressing room. Just as he ushered her to her room, Mikhail appeared out of nowhere. The man didn't even say anything to him, not that he ever did, normally Leo took his orders from Abram or Krill.

Quickly Leo stepped out of the way to let the man through. Thankfully the bastard didn't close the door all the way, allowing Leo to see somewhat into the tiny room. Though the opening was narrow Leo could see Misha's stunned expression.

Leo just didn't understand Misha's obsession over the guy, though she never said anything it was plain as day that she was infatuated with Mikhail. The man simply wasn't good looking, always wearing that same damned stony expression his face looked as if it were carved out of granite. Not to mention the arctic gaze he fixed on everyone. Misha deserved someone who had style, that could make her laugh, and appreciate her like Leo did.

Leo watched in irritation as Misha fawned over the flowers, but nothing could prepare him for what happened next. Leo's whole body tensed as he watched that bastard kiss her. The face Leo dreamed she would make was coming alive in front of him for another man. Clenching his fist to keep him from doing anything stupid Leo stood motionless as Mikhail left.

Now as he watched her glide gracefully across the room with her ever present smile, Leo began to think about their future. Soon Leo would tell Misha of his feelings.

Chapter 8

After the reception, everyone including Letisha and Jay met at the Rose for a small celebration. Misha was shocked to see that the Rose was closed to customers tonight. Instead of gathering in the back room as she imagined she got to celebrate with everyone in the front part of the restaurant. The place was packed, absolutely everyone was there. Changing in the bathroom into the second dress she brought Misha couldn't stop smiling.

"You look happy," Vera noted.

"I am," Misha grinned at Vera's reflection through the mirror. "I am just so happy to be celebrating this with everyone."

"Well, you should be, because you deserve it. You were amazing tonight. I am just so proud of you."

The last part came out in Russian, Vera probably didn't even realize she switched over, she was too busy trying to covertly dab away the tears in her eyes. Turning around, ignoring the fact her dress was still unzipped, Misha hugged Vera and whispered into her ear.

"I love you, Vera thank you for being the mother I couldn't have. Thank you for everything." Vera's grip around Misha's back tightened in response before pulling away suddenly.

"Damn you for trying to mess up my make-up, now turn around so I can finish."

After changing she stepped back out into the noisy, crowded front room, blushing at all the men's friendly whistles and catcalls at her reappearance, she quickly shuffled over to the main table. Sitting across from her friends, Misha quickly took her seat between Mikhail and Krill. She wondered if Mikhail noticed her in the dress like the other men did? Though she knew they were just being jovial, a big part of her wanted to see Mikhail look at her again like he did that day in her bedroom. God, she was being juvenile, but all she could think about was the kiss. But he just sat there casually with one elbow on the table talking to Krill.

Though Misha hardly ever seen Mikhail sit in the front of his own restaurant, he looked just as comfortable in the front room as he did in the back. Looking at him casually talk to Krill about business she remembered how Vera once explained to her how the "business" worked.

One day after middle school, sitting in one of the booths at the Rose across from Vera, Misha listened to her explain.

"Well first you must know, Mikhail is vastly different from the usual men in the brotherhood, he doesn't run things like Roman," she looked at her with an expression that gave Misha the impression that meant a lot.

"To begin with, Mikhail is the youngest boss that I know of, and I know he is the youngest Vladamir ever entrusted," Vera said. "Vladamir, you know—the head of the family," she paused to make sure Misha actually knew the name. Misha eagerly nodded.

"Well, he allowed for there to be two bosses in Boston. It was because Mikhail has a special skill when it comes to making money. Unlike most Mikhail only needs two captains, each captain runs a multitude of business sending all the money to Mikhail, which he in turn sends to Vladamir. Though technically Mikhail owns all of the establishments nothing is in his name besides the shipyards of course."

"Oh I think I get it now," Misha replied. Having Vera explain it, all the conversations Misha overheard started to make more sense. Every since she met Mikhail Kulakov, Misha was determined to know everything about the man.

"What are you two ladies over here talking about?" Sitting down his half-empty glass, Nico slid into the booth right next to her, crowding her against the wall and his tall frame. Misha didn't mind. However, she loved talking to Nico. He always made her laugh.

"I was explaining to her how things work around here."

"Ahh I see."

"Nico," Misha started hesitantly. "How long have you been—doing this?"

Taken aback at her question Nico paused for a moment, making her regret her question before he gave her a gentle smirk.

"I have been 'doing this' my whole life little one."

"Even when you were a child?" Misha asked.
Vera and Nico shared a quick depreciating laugh before answering her question.

"There is no such thing of being 'child' in Russia. You are simply younger and smaller, and that's all. Life's cruelty did not and does not discriminate to the children where I come from." Nico took a large swallow of the clear liquid in his glass, before waving down the waitress for another. "Hell, the only thing I can remember about being a kid was being separated from my brothers and thrown into an orphanage."

Out of nowhere the last memories of her siblings popped into Misha's mind. She remembered them crammed together in her mom's beat up Lincoln. She could remember two of her sister's fighting for something on one side of the car while her and three of her older brothers stared out the window calling out stuff they seen. Misha didn't even remember getting out of the car, all she could remember was her mom handing her some money and telling her to wait at the diner.

"Don't cry sweety." Vera's voice broke through her thoughts, she looked down to see Vera's hand covering her clenched fist. Wiping away the tears with her other hand Misha smiled back at Vera. Nico's long arm wrapped around her shoulders, bringing her close to him. She was just opening her mouth to tell them she was OK, but a shadow fell over their booth, looking up they were greeted by Mikhail's stoic presence.

"Its time to go Misha." his cold eyes settled on Nico, making the man promptly release her and stand up to let her out of the booth. After saying her goodbyes to everyone she followed Mikhail to his car.

The ride home was quiet. Normally she would talk pretty much at him since Mikhail didn't really talk a lot, but tonight all she could think about was one thing. After learning a little bit more about Mikhail and hearing Nico's statement about growing up in Russia, Misha wanted to know more about Mikhail's childhood.

Though every time she wanted to ask the man anything, she talked herself out of it out of fear. What if she accidentally made him mad, by asking too many questions or being nosy? It really wasn't her place to ask him anything. Every day she reminded herself to be more than merely grateful, she needed to be completely beholden to the man she owed everything.

Parking in the brightly lit underground garage to their building, Mikhail sat silently. Taking her hand off the door handle, Misha turned to look at Mikhail, to see why he paused.

"Misha," Mikhail began, getting her full attention. "What were you talking about with Nico?"

"Oh," Misha explained carefully. "well he was telling me about how he grew up?"

"And that made you cry?" he turned to look at her with a skeptical glance.

"Yeah sorta," she fiddled with the hem of her pleated school mandated skirt. "His story reminded me of my brothers and sisters." looking up to see what his reaction was, she hastened to continue when she saw that he was still staring at her. "I just felt bad for him, and I guess I felt bad for myself a little."

"Do you miss them?" his voice seemed deeper than usual. It alarmed her.

"No!" she quickly replied. Seeing his eyebrow furrow she tried to explain. "I mean yes, but not like that. I mean I want to stay with you still Mikhail."

"Misha calm down," he sighed, giving her a hard stare. " Saying you miss your siblings will not affect the fact that you belong to me now." The surety in which he said that made her sigh in relief.

"OK," she began again, this time taking a deep breath to get her thoughts together. "I meant that I miss them, and I wonder how there doing, but I feel bad when I think of them because every time I do I only feel so happy that I am with you. I know it sounds selfish and terrible but I only just want to be here."

"There is nothing selfish about knowing what you want," he turned to look out the front window. "That is how I got to where I am today. When I was about your age, my sister was sold off by my stepfather. Soon after that he sold me to a man under Vladimir. I worked and scraped as pretty much a slave until I got the attention of Vladamir. I went back and killed my stepfather and with Vladimir's permission I killed the man who bought my sister."

"Did you save your sister?" she asked, her eyes wide at the implications of his story.

"No" she could hear the anger in his voice. "I didn't get to her in time."

Unbuckling her seat belt Misha climbed to her knees on the leather seat and leaned over and wrapped her arms around his neck. She could feel the constriction of her throat as tears threatened to spill.

"I am sorry," she whispered, her cheek pressed against his. Pulling back a little she watched him turn to face her directly. With her kneeling position, their faces were only inches apart.

"Life handed you and I a shit hand at an early age, so don't ever feel bad to go after what you want."

Nodding vigorously, she followed him out of the car. Everyday since she met Mikhail Kulakov, Misha was thankful. Thankful he seemed to genuinely care about her, thankful he trusted her enough to tell her about his past, and thankful he gave her a future to hope for.

Now as she sat there absently staring at him through her peripheral, doing her best to keep up the conversation with Jay and Letisha, she had to wonder if knowing all that she did how could she still be so surprised by the man even now. Never in her wildest of fantasies would she have imagined Mikhail kissing her or even showing up to her performance. Knowing she would surely start grinning like an idiot if she kept remembering the scene, Misha pushed back the thoughts for later.

After hours of laughter and talking Misha followed Mikhail back into the condo. She was so tired she had to take off her heels in the elevator just to make it any further. Though through her fatigue, it did not escape her notice that this was the first time they have been alone since her dressing room. Though all she wanted to do was mention the kiss. She also prayed he would not mention it, Misha didn't trust her reaction. There was no telling if she would make a fool of herself and confess her love for him or just stare at him like a lost puppy. Too nervous to take a chance she opted for a quick goodnight as she turned down her hallway.

"Are you happy?" the deep accent sliced through the silence.

Turning around she looked at him, he was standing in the middle of the living area with one hand in his pocket looking directly at her, his eyes held an intensity Misha never seen before. Setting the violin on the kitchen bar she stepped closer to him before answering.

"Of course I am happy. I am probably the happiest person in the world right now," she admitted "between doing well at the performance and you attending, there is nothing more I could want." Well maybe another kiss, but Misha would die before mentioning that.

His hand raised as if he was going to touch her shoulder, but he stopped, pulling back as if it were a bad idea.

"Good." Turning Mikhail walked away leaving her confused. Misha got the feeling he stopped himself from saying anything else. Grabbing her violin she made her way to her room.

Standing on his balcony, Mikhail shut his eyes to the crisp breeze. What in the hell was he thinking? Why in God's name did he kiss her? With every question, he asked himself another one followed. Mikhail didn't want to admit what it was that came over him, to grab that slip of pink paper as he headed out of the door to her performance. If he admitted to his growing infatuation with the girl he felt that he would somehow be too far gone. That somehow it would lead to something more dangerous.

Leaning against the cold metal railing, he braced himself on his forearms. It didn't help that he noticed Misha's increasing adoration for him, every time he looked into her eyes his will got a little weaker. Shaking his head, Mikhail couldn't even figure out where all this started or where the hell it was going. One moment everything was fine it was just Misha, the girl that lived under his roof. Now everything was different, he kissed her dammit. Though technically he really wouldn't have considered that a kiss, but with Misha somehow that very brief contact with her soft lips made it feel very much like a kiss. The desire that crackled through him when their lips meet had to be criminal.

Even his renowned control was slipping, just recalling his men reactions to her short gray dress at his restaurant caused him to grip the railing in rage. Of course, she was beautiful Mikhail had to expect that this would happen, but that did nothing to quell his rage. The feeling of grabbing her and hauling her out of the crowded restaurant, from his men eyes was overwhelming.

Unlike his earlier promise to himself, this time he was going to stand firm in his decision. From this moment forward he was going to forget about his "moments" with Misha, he was going to start anew. Mikhail was going to take extra precautions not to put himself in such intimate situations with Misha.

Chapter 9

Sitting cross legged on the plush sofa in her studio Misha listened to Letisha and Jay pass ideas by Krill for their debut at Vital. Like every musically inclined group of friends since the beginning of time, they were in a band. When the three of them meet in high school, it was as if it were ordained by the fates. Each one of them on their own was highly acclaimed in their own right, but when they got together, they broke boundaries.

Letisha was already signed to a moderately well known music label before she graduated high school. Misha could literally feel the jealousy coming from the other girls in their music department. Not that Letisha minded. She was a diva through and through, unfortunately for everyone else she had the vocals to back it up. Jay on the other hand kept his ego under a firmer grasp, despite the fact he freelanced for professional tours and gigs as a backup drummer. Jay could emulate any drum style making him extremely valuable.

Between Jay's knack for beat making, Letisha's lyric writing, and Misha's music composition they were quite a team. Misha's goal was to become one of Boston's exclusive producers, she wanted to work with all kinds of artist making truly one of a kind songs that people would know it was her the moment they listened.

"I will take a look at these dates and email you back," Krill said, as he folded the piece of paper he was scribbling on earlier, stuffing it into his pocket. Stopping at the door, he turned his gaze to her narrowing his eyes, "Misha what do you think your wearing in this weather?"

Caught off guard Misha looked down at her thin purple leggings and pink polka dot sweater in confusion. "What!" she cried, "I am even wearing boots. What's wrong with what I have on?" though she asked the question Misha could pretty much guess his response.

"You know you get sick every year around this time. Why must I tell you to put on warmer clothes?" Krill rarely got mad at her, but she could recognize the early signs of dissatisfaction in his voice.

"I'm sorry," dropping her pen and paper on the couch next to her she ran over to give him an apologetic hug. "I will go home and change into something warmer."

Smiling at his grunt of approval, she waited for him to leave the studio before she turned back to her snickering friends.

Leaving Leo downstairs to smoke, Misha rushed upstairs to change. When she left the studio that morning, a cold gust of wind whipped right through her flimsy tights. Yeah maybe Krill was right. Every year once it hit winter, it brought along two things. First she would get extremely sick, with a flu like sickness. Secondly it meant her birthday wasn't too far off.

Stepping through the front door she turned to run to her room, but the familiar clang of metal changed her course. Curious she crept through the open doorway that led to Mikhail's side of the condo. Following the clanging sound, she slowly approached the open doorway to the gym.

Carefully she pressed herself against the wall as she leaned sideways hoping to catch a glimpse through the crack of the door. Seeing the familiar machines and weights, she scanned the gym for the source of the sounds through the limited opening. Leaning forward a little more she caught the sight of the tattooed star on a large pale knee. Her eyes widened as her heart rate picked up, Misha had only seen the tattoos beneath Mikhail's waist once before. Doing her best to stay quiet as the metal clanked repeatedly from the lifting and dropping of the weights she scanned further up the leg. Due to her position she could only see half his body meaning only one leg was at her disposal but she could see that his thigh held numerous tattoos as well.

Without even realizing it her gaze was boldly traveling up his bare torso across the tight muscles of his abs. Misha watched in breathless silence as the one arm powerfully lifted the bar above his head. Daring to lean a little further she moved until the crack in the door's opening allowed her to see his face--a face pointed directly at her. The moment her eyes clashed with his glacial gaze she panicked. Silently she launched herself away from the wall and rushed silently through the carpeted living room to her room.

Oh my God, did he see her? Please God, she prayed, please let that just been a coincidence. Could he have really seen her through the crack in the door into a dark hallway? Surely not. But she couldn't get the image of his burning look out of her mind.

Quickly she went to her closet to grab some jeans, she needed to get out of here as quickly as possible.

"Hey sweetheart you still changing?" the familiar flirtatious voice rang down her hallway, ruining her intention to escape quietly.

Still buttoning her pants she flew to her door to shush Leo. But it was too late. Leo realized it too. Misha froze as she watched Mikhail walk barefoot down the hallway towards the frozen Leo. Mikhail didn't look angry by the disturbance from what Misha could see nor did his eyes hold the glimmer of amusement either. Dressed only in shorts Mikhail's tall form glistened with sweat as he walked right past the still Leo.

Without turning his head to look at his soldier, he voiced his command in Russian, "Wait outside."

With a quick nod, Leo spared her a quick glance before he stepped into the small entry hall to the elevator shutting the door behind him.

Misha swallowed silently as Mikhail continued towards her. Why did she go down that darn hallway? Stopping only a few feet away from her she hesitantly looked up. His gaze narrowed as he fixed it on her still frozen hands. Looking down she realized she still had her hands clutched tightly onto the buttons of her still open fly.

Blushing like mad she quickly fumbled until she had them fastened "Sorry." she mumbled.

Mikhail said nothing.

Nervously she tried to fill the silence. "I am sorry that we disturbed your workout Mikhail, it will never--,"

Stepping closer she felt his hand firmly grasp the back of her neck. The sense of power radiating through his grip silenced her effectively. "Make sure you wear a scarf," gently she felt his thumb caress the length of her throat. "I don't want you getting sick again."

Releasing his grasp he stepped back, giving her an expectant look. Mentally shaking herself out of the daze he caused she nodded before escaping into her room for said scarf. Wrapping the scarf tightly around her neck, she came back out of her room only to find Mikhail closing the front door and walking back towards the gym.

Out in the entrance hall, Leo stood with a grave face.

"I am so sorry Leo I didn't know he would be home," she said soothingly as she approached the blonde haired man. "I think I made him angry by disturbing him. I hope you didn't get in trouble because of me. If so, please let me know and I can--,"

"No," Leo pressed the button for the first floor, "you didn't do anything. The boss just didn't like my familiarity with you."

"Oh you mean calling me 'sweetheart,'" she concluded. Hooking her arm through Leo's, she leaned her head on his shoulder. "Don't worry about it, you know how serious Mikhail can be. Besides I still want us to have a good time today. After you taking those online classes for what seems like ever, I am excited to see your photography skills at work."

Instantly his face brightened, pulling his arm tighter he pressed her arm closer. "You're right, today we won't even think of the boss."

Chapter 10

Her body was hot, her throat was sore, and her head felt as if was going to explode—she was sick. Unlike the times before however no one knew.

"You look pitiful," Leo's laughing voice rang somewhere over her head.

Well, Leo knew, but no one else knew. Thankfully Mikhail and Krill were out of town for some sort of meeting. So instead of enduring their critical looks, this year she was going to get off Scot-free. If it didn't hurt to move, she would laugh manically.

"Shut up, you said you were going to help me today." she tried to keep the whine out of her voice but she was too weak.

Feeling the cold shock of the damp rag swipe across her hot forehead, she groaned in satisfaction. "Oh my God Leo that feels great," she mumbled from beneath her purple and white sheets she was currently buried within. Cracking open an eye, she was a little taken aback by the shadow that seemed to cross his eyes.

Before she could say anything, he replaced the hooded look with his signature flirtatious smile. Sitting at the edge of her bed next to her Leo leaned over her.

"I am glad," he declared, "can't have my future wife neglected now can I?"

Smiling at his secret title for her she sank deeper into her pillow, her head was beginning to swim a little.

"Unlike most men," he continued to drag the cold rag down her neck, "I make sure that the woman in my life is number one."

Through the growing fever, Misha's mind raced in abandon. Memories of Mikhail's attitude of late popped into her mind. Whether she was at the office or visiting the Rose, Mikhail snapped at everyone around her. She was afraid of asking the bartender for a soda in fear he would glare at the poor man. Even before he left, he growled at her at the shipyards. She was simply giving Michael a hug, something she did nearly every morning for the past couple of years, but Mikhail reprimanded him for not being on the docks, sending Michael rushing away from her as if she were plagued. The icy look he gave her every time he snapped just confused her more. She wasn't sure what she was doing to make him so mad. If she weren't so sick, she would have probably dwelled on it until she was sick anyway.

The sudden shock of cold hitting her chest shook her out of her thoughts. Looking down she watched in a numbing trance as Leo's tattooed hand drug the rag across her chest. Somehow the buttons to her night shirt were open revealing the expanse of her chest. If he moved any further, he would touch her breast.

She wanted to tell him he has done enough, to stop him from going any further, but she was so dizzy and weak the sounds that came out were unintelligible.

Leaning down until he was directly above her, face to face, he looked into her heavy lidded eyes. "What did you say, sweetheart?"

Misha wasn't sure if it was her fever or what, but the look in Leo's eyes bordered a strange excitement. He must have seen the confusion in her eyes because thankfully he stood up.

"Let me go get you some tea."

Walking through the front door, Mikhail immediately realized something was off. The air seemed strange. Not to mention there was a black glock sitting on his kitchen counter. Standing still he listened. Muted murmurs came from Misha's bedroom, one light and feminine the other annoyingly familiar. Silently he stepped to the side of the living room blocked from the kitchen's view and watched undetected as Leo walked into his kitchen. With narrowed eyes, he watched the younger man grab a mug from his cabinet and start the electric tea kettle.

The man's casualness in his home made him recall Krill's earlier statement. Sitting in the jet on their way to the meeting with Roman in New York, Krill voiced his concerns about Leo.

Leaning forward in his seat Krill looked across the small table towards him,"You know I never liked the kid?"

Mikhail nodded silently.

"But I know he worked hard to earn back his trust with us and for a moment there I thought he was perfect for watching after my Misha," Krill rasped, Mikhail could see his growing agitation as he explained. Staying silent Mikhail listened.

"But I don't think he is right for the job anymore. He is getting too close."

"Close?" Mikhail asked carefully.

"Yes dammit," Krill grumbled, "Every day I see him, I see the way he looks at her, the way he hangs around her as if they were friends. The kid is not there to make friends with her dammit! He is getting too familiar with her."

Leaning back Mikhail absorbed the information. He too has caught Leo's familiarity with Misha. Just recalling his use of "sweetheart" annoyed him. Though Mikhail made sure Leo would never use such a term again if he valued his tongue.

"So what would you like to do?" he asked calmly.

"I am thinking of changing her guard."

And here it was the crux of the problem. With a small smile, he leaned over to stare unseeingly out the window."I take it you want me to be the one to inform Misha?"

"You know how she can be when she defends her 'friends.'" Mikhail could feel the captain's beseeching gaze.

"I will think about it."

At first, despite Leo's egregious error, Mikhail figured it was just Krill's overprotective nature towards Misha that caused him to be concerned. Though, looking at the man in his kitchen gave Mikhail pause to think.

Figuring it was time to reveal himself, Mikhail stepped forward.

Everything felt like a dream. Misha's arms and legs felt like lead weights, she could barely move to get comfortable. Staring out of the large windows, she could only see the tops of the skyscrapers in the distance from her position. Smiling she remembered how in awe she was when Mikhail told her she could stay. That night she hardly slept, she just remembered staring out of the windows at the lights of the city.

A fit of coughs brought her back to the present. Where was Leo? Closing her eyes, she drifted off for a second until she heard footsteps coming into her room.

"I was wondering what happened to you?" she mumbled turning over.

Holding a cup of what Misha could only assume was her missing tea, was Mikhail's large very foreboding figure.

"Were you now?" setting the cup down on her nightstand, Mikhail sat on the edge of her bed, the same spot Leo sat earlier. She could tell by the way his jaw was set and the way his hard blue eyes seemed to burn a whole right through her, that he was angry.

"What happened to Leo?" she whispered, trying to avoid his icy stare.

"I sent him home." His gaze seemed to linger on the flesh that was peeking out of her shirt, the spot Leo wiped down earlier. Misha could practically see Mikhail put the pieces together in his head.

"Mikhail I..."

Cutting her off her cupped her face with his large cool hand, turning her face into his callused hand Misha nearly moaned at the refreshing touch. Gently he swiped his thumb across her lips.

"Misha, from now on Leo is never to come into my home," his unrelenting gaze pinned her down, "Understood?"

Why could he not come in? Why was Mikhail being so mean lately? What was going on? All of these were questions swimming through her head, but she was too tired to voice them. In defeat, she closed her eyes and nodded.

Hearing nothing else Misha assumed he was going to leave, unfortunately she was wrong. With a cold whoosh, the blankets she was buried beneath were thrown off. Shocked her eyes snapped open, to see Mikhail standing above her before she could react she felt his hands slip beneath her legs and shoulders. Hauling her up into his arms Misha felt her head spin.

"Mikhail!" she cried softly,"what are doing?"

"You're burning up, I am going to have to cool you down."

Putting the clues together, Misha tried to wriggle free from his hold. "No Mikhail, no please I'm fine..."

"Hush." he growled, his grip tightened almost painfully stilling her struggles.

Clutching onto his shoulder the best she could, Misha watched in a daze as he carried her into his room. God, she never felt so embarrassed in her life. Setting her on the bed Mikhail stepped back and walked to his dresser. Flicking the clasp on his watch, he tossed the gold piece onto the dresser. Next he removed his shoes, his socks, and then his shirt. In a state of awe, she could only sit and watch his movements. Wearing nothing but his black slacks Mikhail turned back to her. She couldn't believe this was happening.

The knot in her stomach twisted in fear and anticipation as he approached her side. Without warning, he reached for her shirt and began unbuttoning. On instinct, her hands flew up to stop him but he seemed to expect her move. Catching her hands, he gave her a warning glare. By now she was breathing so hard her chest was heaving. She was so confused as to why he was doing this, why was he being so rough with her? Mostly though she was nervous for him to see her in only her underwear.

Moving her like a rag doll he completely divested her of the shirt, leaving her only in her cotton blue underwear. There was no time to cover herself in modesty, picking her back up he headed for the large shower. Misha pressed her face into his chest in apprehension. Despite being dizzy from her fever, she knew what he was going to do.

Stepping into the shower, he released her legs so that she could stand against him. Quickly he turned on the cold spray.

The moment the cold water hit her hot skin she yelped in shock. Yanking back she tried to escape the torturous temperature.

"Dammit Misha stop." he ordered harshly has he pushed her against the wall in water's spray.

By now she was not only miserable, embarrassed beyond words, she was enraged. Letting out a frustrated growl she began to fight off his grip.

"No you stop!" she yelled, "Let me go, this is archaic." twisting out of his slick grip she tried to push out of the shower door. Rough hands savagely grabbed her, yanking backwards against his soaked body. Pivoting easily on his heel he turned until she was directly facing the spray. With her arms in a vice grip behind her, Misha hung her head in defeat. Exhausted she sank heavily against him. Releasing her arms, he encircled his arms around her as she endured the spray.

"I'm sorry my little Misha." the deep vibrations from his chest spread throughout her body. Closing her eyes, everything went to black for a moment. The next thing she remembered was being carried soaking wet into his bedroom. She felt the cool sheets hit the back of her head as she felt a warm towel pass over her body. With each pass of the towel, she felt her body jiggle and sway to his rhythm. Through heavy-lidded eyes, she watched the man who she owed her life to dry her off. Maybe it was the fever or the heavy fatigue but she could have sworn something crossed his eyes when he looked at her.

A shiver ran through her leaving goosebumps up and down her body.

"Shit," he cursed, "we need to get you out of the wet clothes."

"You mean my underwear." she drawled drunk with exhaustion.

Clenching his jaw tighter he fixed her a dangerous look. "Yes. I need you to remove them. I will step out--"

"I can barely move," she cut him off. It was true, even if she liked the glimmer of shock that crossed his face, she was too tired to even move. Ha! That's what he gets for tossing her into a cold shower against her will. "I will warm up as soon as I get my pajamas."

"As I said," his voice was dangerously low and dark as he threw the towel over her prone figure. "You need to get out of these wet clothes." With one knee on the bed, Mikhail slipped his hands beneath the towel he placed.

"No Mikhail wait." but it was too late she could feel him hooking his fingers around her panties. With wide eyes, Misha stared directly into the blue storms of his eyes as he drug the wet fabric down her legs and from underneath the towel.

Mikhail watched in no less than fascination as she bit her lip to keep from making a sound. So much for his vow of not putting himself in intimate "moments" with her, and damn did he try. The smooth feeling of her legs gliding across his fingers etched itself into his brain. Scooting forward until he was right beside her, staring down at her he went deeper down the rabbit hole. Ignoring her continued protest he reached underneath her torso to find the clasp of the soaked bra. Expertly he undid the clasp and with a quick tug down her body he removed the bra much in the same way he removed the purple panties.

Stepping back he admired the deep flush to her face before turning back to his bathroom. Closing the door, he quickly changed out of the soaking pants into a pair of track pants and a t-shirt. Pausing for a moment before opening the door, Mikhail leaned his forehead against the door as the thoughts of what he just did flooded his mind. Never did he imagine the reaction Misha's body would cause. So sweet and soft, her body was like silk, and now she was laying completely naked on his bed, guarded by one solitary towel. Gripping the doorknob with fierce control, Mikhail walked back into the bedroom.

Asleep with her head to the side, he couldn't help but stare for a couple of moments. She was so damn trusting. She had no idea the amount of white hot discipline he was summoning right now. Not to climb on the bed with her and explore what has been hidden under his roof the whole time. Cradling her in his arms he began to walk back to her room. Her body temperature felt much better now, archaic, but it worked. Mikhail needed to get her out of his room before he did something stupid. Placing her under her covers, his heart lurched at the tiny feminine moan she made. Grabbing the soggy towel he gently pulled it from underneath her and the covers, leaving her naked beneath.

Now it was he who felt that had the fever, his whole body was on fire with want. Want for his beautiful little Misha. Scratching his head he roughly raked over the stubble, though what he saw earlier he could safely say there was nothing little about Misha anymore. When he pulled off the soaking bra, his hands quickly sensed the beautiful weight of her full breast. The deep flair of her hips reminded him of the nice plump ass that he tried not to notice everyday. Misha was the embodiment of temptation under is roof.

"Mikhail," the light groan caused him to pause. Looking over to the bed she looked at him with heavily lidded eyes. "please don't be mad at Leo. He is my friend." the rest of her words faded as he watched her fall deeper into sleep.

With a low growl of frustration, he walked out of her room making his way towards his liquor cabinet. With his hand on the bottle neck he paused, lower inhibitions and relaxed judgment is not what he needed right now.

Falling back onto his couch Mikhail let out a weary sigh. Pushing the thoughts of forbidden lust out of his mind, he focused on anger. Leo Maslak was flirting with death—again. Seconds after sitting down on Misha's bed Mikhail was able to piece together the earlier scene. The mere fact that he dared to touch her led Mikhail to believe Krill might have a point.

America must be making him soft, he thought in disgust. If this were Russia, hell if this were him eleven years ago, Mikhail would have killed Leo the first time he crossed the line. Though Misha chose to forgive and forget, Mikhail never forgot the kid's transgression.

Misha was still in middle school when Leo was sent over from Roman. Sitting in the back room of the Rose, Mikhail was absently listening to the kid brag about himself and his so called accomplishments. Abram was asking the kid, who had to be twenty-one, some questions as to why he wanted to switch to Mikhail's men. Glancing at his watch Mikhail could really care less about the whole situation, he was only still at the Rose because Nico was picking Misha up from her late night violin class.

"I think I would be better suited for your setup sir," Leo droned doing his best to try and impress the two older men. "Security, cars, running shipments anything you--"

"She is here." Abram perked up, he too seemed bored with the conversation, flicking his thumb behind him, Mikhail looked past the confused Leo to see Misha walk in the door. Immediately the familiar jingle of her backpack jostling started to come towards their table.

"Move," Mikhail commanded, looking at the kid in front of him.

"Yes sir." quickly he got up and stood anxiously by the table.

"You can go kid," Abram drawled, "I will talk to Roman tomorrow." Seeing that he was no longer able to pitch his case Leo nodded before walking towards the bar.

"Hi Abram Hi Mikhail," the high pitched chirp brought both men attention back to the table. Misha smiled brightly, standing in her school uniform while clutching her practice violin. "Are you busy?"

Abram pulled the chair out signaling she could join them, smiling she sat down. That was all Misha needed, once she was seated her entire day's story began. Signaling to the waitress Mikhail quickly ordered Misha's food as she delved into the throes of middle school drama. If someone would have told him years ago, he and his captain would be sitting here trying to keep up with this rapid pace story he would have laughed. Thankfully she paused to excuse herself to the restroom, allowing both men a breather.

Making sure she was halfway across the room, Abram leaned back in his chair with a deep exhale.

"Oh my God how does Krill do this?" Abram laughed quietly, "I mean she is thorough. She just took us from her first class to lunch, to gym. Dammit man, I think there is more."

"Yes well I frankly don't feel bad for you," Mikhail grumbled as he scanned the room absently. "I hear these stories every time I go home."

"Why do you do it?" The laughter faded from Abram's eyes as he looked at him. No one else would dare ask him that question, but Abram was different, Mikhail knew the man had no ill intentions.

"At first it was boredom, then it was refreshing to have such a light to come home to, now it's more of--"

"Of an annoyance." Abram grinned.

Smirking slightly Mikhail continued. "Sometimes she can be a little much, but no, now she is more like," pausing he searched for the perfect word. "now she is more like a radio."

The loud laugh Abram released, quieted the noisy room in shock for a moment before picking back up. Mikhail smirked in response as he looked back towards the back hall. Furrowing his brow, he glanced at the waitress bringing the food. Misha should be back by now. As if on cue he watched her petite figure emerge from the back hall. Something was wrong. Walking slowly towards him her face didn't have its usual glowing smile. Her eyes seemed to be wide in shock while she nibbled on her bottom lip.

Sitting upright in alert Abram must have sensed her strange demeanor as well when she finally sat down. Silently she picked up her fork and began to eat, staring at her plate. Mikhail looked to Abram to see him just as alarmed. Nothing silenced Misha.

"Misha what's wrong?"

Looking up from her plate she gave him a forced smile. "It's nothing I'm just hungry."

Taking a deep breath, Mikhail reminded himself he was dealing with a child. Leaning back in his chair he stared at her for a moment.

"Misha come here." Tapping the empty chair to his left. Obediently she got up and walked around the table. Sitting down next to him she hesitantly looked up at him, her large eyes were like windows to her emotions, he could see the hurt and worry inside of them. Draping one arm on the back of her chair, he gently grabbed her chin.

"I am going to ask you one more time. And I want the truth, Misha. What happened?" he asked evenly.

By now he could sense the quiet spreading through the room, others must have noticed them. Like tiny needles spreading through his body, Mikhail watched as moisture built up in her eyes.

"I was about to come out of the bathroom when I heard someone talking about me through the door." Mikhail listened in complete stillness.

"He said I ruined everything for him, and he called me some bad names."

"What did he say? Who was it?" Abram questioned.

Mikhail cast a murderous glance to Abram before turning back to Misha. "Tell me."

Quietly Misha repeated the vile words she heard before describing the blonde haired kid standing near the back hall entrance. Doing his best not to kill the fucker then and there, Mikhail calmly signaled for Nico.

"I want you to get your things and go with Nico," he spoke evenly, "he is going to get you something to eat and take you home."

"I am sorry Mikhail I didn't know--" holding up his hand he silenced the oncoming tears.

"Misha not another word, I need you to go."

Nodding she grabbed her things and followed Nico out. Once the door closed, Mikhail nodded at Abram. Immediately Abram snapped his fingers at two of his men he pointed to Leo. The kid never had a chance to react before he was thrown out of his chair and drug across the room. The men parted like the red sea as they drug the now yelling blonde across the room, by now everyone in the room was on their feet.

Snatching his phone out of his pocket, Mikhail called Roman never taking his eyes off the yelling offender. Listening to it ring he held his hand over the phone and leaned forward.

"Shut up." Mikhail calmly commanded, immediately Leo stopped struggling. Being held face down on the table Leo stared at him with wide eyes.

Finally, Roman's voice came over the line, Mikhail put him on speaker.

"Roman its Mikhail, let me inform you personally of the actions of a the piece of shit you sent over." Never taking his eyes off Leo's, he described to Roman, as his men listened, what Leo said about Misha. Mikhail took some pride in the fact that he could see the outrage wash over his men at Misha's treatment.

"My apologies Mikhail," Normally Roman found everything either very funny or very displeasing. The man was either always laughing or yelling at someone or something. So the remorseful tone held weight with Mikhail. "I would have never sent the fuck over if I knew he was capable of something like this. Despite the fact, he is dumb and cocky the kid is very good at talking himself out and into difficult situations. He has made all my deals with the 3-6 Machetes, and those Mexican fucks are insane. So keep him as a slave or kill him, that's my gift to you."

Somehow Leo paled even more so.

Hanging up the phone Mikhail tossed it onto the table, with a nod he signaled for the two men to release Leo. The rest of his men formed a sort of semi-circle around them. Nervously Leo shifted his weight from each leg, he looked as if he wanted to bolt any minute, Mikhail kind of wished he would just so he could put a bullet in the back of his fucking head.

Pulling out his gun he kept in his back waistband, Mikhail pulled the black gun around pointing it at the now shaking blonde. At the sight of the gun, the kid shuffled back until he hit the bar counter.

"You come to my place, and you insult the only person in this room who couldn't defend herself." with each word Mikhail could feel his anger growing becoming more chaotic. It was nostalgic in a way, the last time he was this angry he threw two men into an oncoming train. But that was before he came to America, that was before he was able to experience the simple joy of mundane everyday life.

"Wait, sir, let me..."

The sound of the gun cocking silenced Leo.

"You come to me with the arrogance to assume I was going to let you into my crew so easily and then get angry when you were told to just...fucking...wait." The overflowing anger reverted his speech into Russian. With every word the men surrounding them voiced their agreement, some even shouted to kill him.

"If you survive you will work for both captains as their slave. You will work without pay as long as I see fit. You will sleep on the floor of Abram's garage. And if you survive the winter on the floor of the garage and decide to step out of line again, you won't have to worry about me killing you. I will simply make a call and have you shipped to a camp deep in mother, Russia. Where I will be ensured to know

that you will literally be fucked for the rest of your sorry life."
Mikhail punctuated the sentence by squeezing the trigger.

The reverberating sound of the gunshot mixed with Leo's scream
filled the back room of the Rose, thankfully they were closed.
Mikhail watched as Leo grasped at his bleeding stomach while
sinking to the floor.

Grabbing his phone off the table, he walked past the laughing men.
"Someone call Isaac."

Unfortunately, the kid survived the shot, and somehow survived
years of Abram and Krill's maniacal slavery. Despite their intentions,
Leo actually proved very useful and due to a scheduling conflict Leo
was made Misha's driver one day.

Mikhail wasn't even sure why he was worried as to how she would
react seeing Leo, everything for Misha was water under a bridge.
She came into his office that day smiling and laughing with the
blonde as if nothing ever happened. But now the friendship he
allowed was starting to cause problems.

Mikhail rarely regretted anything, but he should have killed Leo
from the start.

Chapter 11

With both arms stretched to the length of the back of the couch, Mikhail leaned his head back to stare at the ceiling of the darkened room and wondered how he got to this point. With only the flickering of the TV's lights across the room, the slight weight of Misha's head on his in his lap prompted him to recall the morning's events.

Sitting in his office, Mikhail found himself staring at the security feed of Misha's studio. This was not an unusual habit, every now and then he would take a look to see what she was doing or where were her whereabouts. But this morning in light of last week's event he was just staring at the monitor absently. Without thinking, he called her on her cell phone and informed her of his plans, after watching her face light up, she gathered her things, he met her at his car.

What in the hell inspired him to act like a complete idiot and play hooky on the day he was expecting a large shipment from the Colombians was beyond him. Though he would admit, the evening had been nice. For once in what seemed like forever Mikhail got to relax in his own home. The type of relaxation he knew he wouldn't get again for quite a while. Vladamir was keeping him very busy. For the next few months, he will be expecting weekly weapons shipments. Probably for the first time in weeks he sat down at the barstool in his kitchen for longer than twenty minutes. Tonight was special, he got not only to see but bask in another side of Misha—her domestic side.

He watched her prepare dinner while conversing with him in ease. Watching her handle herself in the kitchen brought an odd sense of comfort. He teased her with memories of her cooking failures when she was younger while learning from the kitchen staff at the Rose. Mikhail realized he loved the way she scrunched up her face when she was embarrassed. Sadly he was starting to realize he liked a lot of things about Misha. Hell, it was taking extreme discipline to try and forget the night he undressed her.

Even now as she lay on his lap breathing evenly as they watched the movie he couldn't stop his eyes from roaming. Unfortunately for him tonight her attire was a little out of the norm. The orange sweater still looked as if she raided a thrift store from the eighties, but it was shorter than all the others. This one didn't fall to her hips like all the others, and it sat high on her waist accompanied by electric blue tights.

And God were they tight. To both Krill and his chagrin, they realized early on in Misha's development she was not going to be average looking. No, the fates just couldn't let him have that. Misha filled out everywhere it counted. By high school her destined curvy figure was coming out in full force. Thankfully she had a predilection for the eighties fashion, and that meant big hair and baggy clothing. All of which Krill was immensely thankful.

Laying on her side, he was allowed full access to the outline of her round ass. Thick, firm thighs tapered gently at her knees before flaring into strong calves. Pulling his gaze back up her body he let his gaze rest on the slender neck resting on his thigh. He fought and won the urge to touch the soft skin.

The muffled sound of television gunfire hardly registered as he sat there watching the rise and fall of her shoulder. Mikhail didn't even need to look to know that she was asleep. Checking his watch he winced at the time. There were five shipments coming in tomorrow that required him being present.

"Misha," he nudged her shoulder. With the greatest interest, he watched her slowly sit up. "Go to your room."

Still sitting on the couch, Misha stared at him through half lidded eyes as he stood up to leave.

"No, I want to sleep with you." Slowly he turned to see her staring at him, her eyes were hazy with fatigue, but her brow furrowed in intent.

"You what?" surely he misheard.

"Mikhail," she whined as she plopped backward onto the couch, the abrupt position caused the sweater to ride high baring her smooth skin of her stomach. "Why can't we do this all the time, I had so much fun today I don't want you to leave me."

"So sleeping with me is your solution?" though he shouldn't even broach the topic he felt a sick sort of curiosity to hear her answer.

"Well, maybe not sleep together per se," by now she was fully awake as she slowly sat back up to reevaluate her request. "But you know, I meant--I just mean I didn't want it to end."

"Its three in the morning Misha, we have been together since lunch," he said flicking at his watch. Her face immediately looked contrite. With her head down she got up and grabbed her blanket she was laying on.

"I am sorry," she whispered in a low voice. She couldn't believe how selfish she was being, after all that he did for her today she was still asking for more. Looking up she was startled to hear the TV shut off causing the room to go pitch black. Her heart sank a little as she took that as his cue of dismissal.

Since her eyes didn't get a chance to adjust to the little bit of night light coming through the windows, she carefully felt her way around the couch towards her room. She felt as if she might have been halfway across the room when she felt strong arms suddenly wrap around her waist pulling her into a hard body.

"Dammit Misha." the familiar growl in her ear made her whole body shiver. The short sweater she was wearing rode up higher allowing her to feel his hands on her bare waist. Misha shut her eyes to the feeling of her butt pressed against his hard thighs while his face was pressed against the side of hers.

"I am so sorry, please don't be..."

"Shut up." The harsh command paired with the rough grip on her arm immediately silenced her. Still blinded by the darkness, Misha felt herself being pulled in the opposite direction. She felt herself being led through the open door of his hallway. The grip on her arm disappeared once they entered his dimly lit room. Only the light from the open bathroom door illuminated the masculine room. Realizing she was still holding her blanket like a child, she quickly draped it on the closest chair. Misha had no idea what was going on all she knew was that her heart was beating wildly. To be alone with Mikhail in his bedroom, at night, no less was a nonexistent occurrence. This was something only her fantasies conjured up.

Pulling a drawer open she watched as he grabbed a shirt, before tossing it to her.

"You can wear this." It was more of a command than a gesture. Not giving her time to answer he walked into his bathroom and shut the door.

Shocked and so dearly confused Misha stood frozen for five seconds before she realized he was going to come back out expecting her changed. Like the wind, she divested herself of her clothes and changed into the wonderful smelling shirt. Nothing compared to Mikhail's scent, it drove her senses crazy.

As expected Mikhail came out of the bathroom completely changed, wearing breezy cotton pants and nothing else. Misha could feel herself staring like an idiot. Pulling back the covers she watched him slide into the large bed, then looked at her. She was still standing in the exact same place wearing the t-shirt that barely touched her knees.

"You said you wanted to sleep with me," he waved his hand over the bed, "so what are you waiting for?"

At that moment, she died a little bit. Not believing this was happening, she slowly climbed up onto his bed and slid underneath the soft covers. Though she was probably the farthest away from him the bed could allow, she was shaking like crazy. Only in her dreams has she thought of herself in this position, but now that she was here in real life she never felt more unsure in her life. Mikhail was a man, a large dangerous man, just knowing that his large frame was lying next to her in bed was making it hard to breathe. Stiffly she turned her head to take a peek at him. Blue eyes and a large smile was waiting for her.

"Bit off a little more than you could chew huh?" it was rare to see Mikhail smile. It usually meant he was in a dangerous mood, or he was laughing at her expense. At this point, she honestly couldn't tell which it was.

Trying to hold back a pout she narrowed her eyes. "No its...its just that it's a little weird for me. I have never been--in--your bed before."

Something dark passed through his eyes before he let out a heavy sigh. Falling onto his back, she felt his arm snake around her waist. Pulling her close, until she was pressed against his side, Misha carefully laid her head on the only place she could, his arm.

"No, you're right to feel this way," his deep accented voice was laced with fatigue, "and technically you really shouldn't be here now."

"I can le..." the powerful arm beneath her curled tighter forcing her to lay partially on his chest.

"No for this one night we can have this."

Looking directly into his blue eyes, Misha was entranced. Not tired at all Misha took the opportunity of her new position to do something she has been wanting to do for years. Relaxing her clenched fist, she let her hands splay softly on his muscular chest. The deep purr like reaction emboldened her as she examined the ink on his body. Just below his nipple she traced the Cyrillic letters.

"Mikhail." she whispered, never taking her eyes off the firm skin beneath her fingertip.

"Mmmm"

"Why did you take me in?" It was a question that she thought of every day but dare never to ask. Tonight, however, the question seemed to roll out of her mouth before she could even think about it.

"Misha" he growled exasperated. "You know why."

Normally she would apologize and immediately retract the question, but this time she stayed vigilant. Still halfway leaning on his chest, she stared at his shut eyes and waited. Finally, his unwavering blue gaze meet hers again.

Seeing she wasn't going to let up he sighed in defeat before letting his hand that was somewhat beneath her, come up and rest on the curve of her back. The heavy weight pressing her flush against his naked torso.

"I took you in to save you and to save me." he looked at her with such blatant honesty, the answer gave her pause to think.

"Did I?"

"Did you what?"

"Did I save you?" she whispered, needing desperately to know if she at least did that, for this man she owed her life to. The hand on her waist slid up her back and buried itself into her loose hair while his eyes became dark with some uncharted emotion.

"You saved a part of me," her heart lurched at his words, she swear it didn't beat, "but you're destroying the rest of me."

Her heart never got a chance to react in pain, before the hand in her hair gripped her hair tightly and pulled her head back to his desire. Strong lips crashed against hers as his body turned and nearly switched their positions. The crushing weight of his body felt so beautifully alarming to the one part of her mind that wasn't stunned.

Pulling away from her swollen lips he looked down at her with the fiercest expression she had ever seen.

"You're starting to seep into my mind," he growled. "Everything about you I never noticed, or purposely tried not to notice is starting to kill me. It's becoming harder and harder to ignore you." With each word, she felt his large hands glide over her body. Even with the thin layer of the shirt couldn't stop her from feeling the heat of his caress.

Distantly she heard herself moan at the feeling of his hands glide just underneath her breast. With a low growl, Mikhail dipped his head until his face was planted directly in the swell of her covered breast. The sharp feeling of his teeth nipping at her breast caused her to cry out.

The moment the sound escaped her lips, it was as if a trance was broken. Pulling away from her as if burned Mikhail sat up onto his heels. Rubbing his hand over his face, he looked at her with pain and guilt.

"What the fuck am I doing? You shouldn't be in here?" he groaned. "God you're just a kid."

A black hole seemed to form at the pit of her stomach as she watched him leave. Startled and partly in shock she slowly slipped from the tall bed and padded to the living room. The spot his keys normally sat was empty. The last time she felt pain like this was when she thought she was being kicked out. She didn't understand what happened. One moment, her dreams were coming true the next—her nightmares. Settling onto her own bed, she let the tears fall.

Chapter 12

No one said anything about the tangible tension surrounding the two. No one knew why Misha stopped talking to the boss. But what Leo did know, is that this was his moment. Between the new blonde broad Mikhail was supposedly dating and Misha's ongoing silent vow towards Mikhail, there was no better time than now.

It had been nearly two weeks now since everyone noticed Misha's seclusion. From what Leo could gather, Mikhail no longer ate breakfast with Misha. Now Leo was taking Misha to and from the studio, which she marched straight to and from, no more midday lunches or breaks in Mikhail's office. Leo couldn't be happier with the turn of events though the same could not be said for Misha.

Sitting in the chair next to her in the studio, Leo watched her focus intently on the laptop screen. Right now she was in the middle of editing music, something she normally would chat through while doing. Today, like the past few days, she remained dead silent as she worked. When she wasn't buried in her music all she did was eat and sleep, she was like a robot. Leo could tell it was worrying her friends, not to mention Krill.

Leo heard from some other guys that Krill had a rather loud conversation with Mikhail, and it wasn't Krill who was yelling. Everyone was shocked, and a little worried, to hear that Mikhail raised his voice, and to Krill no less. Mikhail Kulakov never yelled, he simply acted. From what he could piece together, Krill supposedly confronted Mikhail over his ongoing fight with Misha. But instead of listening to his captain yell and complain as per usual, Mikhail completely shut Krill down. Krill supposedly left very pissed.

Looking at the intense expression on her pretty oval face just seemed wrong somehow. Leo couldn't be happier with the opportunity to pry himself into her heart, but he needed her to focus on him and not her sadness.

"Come on let's go," taking the headphones off of her head he turned her chair around to face him.

"What are you doing, I need to work..." her voice sounded angry, but her eyes held a sense of defeat Leo was growing tired of seeing. Her face should be the full of light and excitement, not sadness from that asshole.

"We are going to go get hot chocolate," he interrupted. Tossing her coat, he watched her contemplate putting it on, finally with a sigh she slowly slipped her arms through the beige suede jacket.

The drive to the coffee shop was silent, just as all the rides as of late. On one hand, Leo couldn't love this fight between Misha and Mikhail more, but on the other hand it was actually making his progress with Misha harder. It was easier to get her to notice him when she would actually talk and not stay trapped in her mind.

Bringing their drinks to the corner table, he picked out Leo sat with his back against the wall. So he could not only see all the exits, but also so they could have some privacy in the corner.

"So are you going to tell me what's going on," he paused smiling devilishly. "Or am I supposed to suffer this in ignorance with everyone else?"

"Nothing is going on," she looked out the window. "Mikhail and I have just reached a different point in our...relationship," she choked out the last word, it nearly burned her throat to utter the word.

What was going on now between them is not what she would define a relationship. Misha wanted the ground to swallow her whole, anything to escape the onslaught of emotions. Regret consumed her for letting her pride destroy the one part of their relationship they did have, their friendship. But her pride burned forever bright, not allowing her to forget the way he left her on his bed looking the fool. The way the new dumb blonde woman pranced happily at his side, while she pined away on the side. Though she told herself every day to get over him, that it simply wasn't meant to be, she couldn't help herself as her eyes wandered up to his office window or across the living room to his door. The pain of her foolishness for the man was eating her alive.

The warm feeling of Leo's hand grabbing her nearly made her release the tears she had been saving for her nights. For the longest she seemed to just stare at the inked hand gently holding hers, she didn't even realize how much she needed the comfort. Grabbing his hands, she smiled brightly for him.

"There is that smile I have been missing," he soothed. "Tonight is the debut of your new song with that fairy, you should be thinking about that, not the boss."

"Oh my God will you stop calling Johnathan a fairy," she pleaded, exasperated by Leo's unwavering dislike for the new artist they were working with.

"Yeah well, anyone who wears jeans that tight deserves whatever name I give him." Leo obviously satisfied with her new mood, propped one foot on the empty seat next to them and lounged back comfortably in his chair.

Laughing at his overall cockiness, she took another sip of her hot chocolate, pushing her thoughts of Mikhail out of her mind for now. "Well, not all guys can be as handsome and stylish as you Leo."

"Don't you forget it."

Dimples, her secret nickname for Johnathan, was talking to her about the performance he just did. The crowd at Vital loved the song, judging not only by their reaction but the I-tunes purchases. Letisha was the first to show her the growing sales on her phone. In what seemed like forever Misha finally smiled in complete joy. The ability to get to taste the success she has been working so hard for was simply euphoric. Not to mention "dimples" was making the moment even better with his flirting. God, he was cute.

Probably under normal circumstances she would never allow herself to laugh and flirt on a private couch of the VIP section with her client. But what the hell. The last few weeks were probably some of the worst in her life, she needed this. Thankfully Vital was designed in the most clever fashion. The large industrial looking nightclub had a large dance floor, a wall to wall bar on one side and a stage on the other. Above the crowd were two loft areas on either side, with two separate stairwells. She and her friends were on one side while management permanently reserved the other side. Management tonight, unfortunately, included Mikhail. Jay warned her Mikhail was here with his new arm candy.

Just thinking of him and this new woman made her inside cringe. No, do not think of him, she commanded herself. She had been doing great all night, refusing to look across the space to catch a peek. He might have made a fool of her before, but she would be damned if he stole all her pride. Taking a deep breath, she smiled even brighter at the cute singer in front of her.

"You look really good tonight by the way." Johnathon leaned in to yell over the music.

"Thank you so much," she wanted to add that Letisha helped her pick out the incredibly tight, not to forget short, white dress. But she just smiled instead.

"So I have been wanting to tell you something," his dimpled smile leaned in closer while his arm slid to the back of the sofa behind her head. Just as he opened his mouth to speak, he was interrupted.

"Misha," Leo's harsh voice cut in between them. "Krill wants you to come see him." She looked up to see his face held a stone hard expression, very unlike the charming Leo.

"Oh ok," carefully she stood up in the insanely tall patent leather white heels which let her reach eye level to Leo, "I will be back," waving at Johnathan before taking Leo's offered arm. Quickly he steered her away from the private booth.

"What's wrong with you?" confused at his menacing attitude. The supportive grip on her waist tightened, as he pushed people out of the way as they walked across the dance floor to the other stairwell.

"I hate that damn dress. I really hate your tall ass shoes. And I fucking despise that fairy fucker hitting on you." he snarled pushing the last person out of the way before leading her safely to the stairwell.

Pausing at the bottom of the stairs Misha stared at him in shock. "Leo you don't have to be so protective, we were just talking, and besides you said I looked good earlier tonight."

"You do look good dammit," he groaned, rubbing the back of his neck in annoyance. "Too damn good to be honest. You have been attracting every fucking dude in here, making my life and job a living hell."

She wanted to apologize, but he was already ushering her up the metal stairs. Getting to the top it hit her, Mikhail was sitting up here with that woman. Finding Krill standing to the side, she walked directly past the large VIP booth Mikhail occupied in the middle. She could feel his dark presence in her peripheral, everything in her body wanted to turn and look at him but dammit she refused.

"My angel you were wonderful." Krill's booming voice was easily heard over the loud music. Hugging the only man she would ever consider a father she smiled.

"I didn't even do anything, we just stood there and watched Johnathan perform." she laughed.

"Nonsense, it was all you that we heard. That boy was nothing but an instrument for you." she couldn't help but blush as he and other men from his crew complimented her work. Turning to thank another compliment, the fates cruelty allowed her to catch a glimpse of Mikhail.

He was staring directly at her.

Her heart nearly fell out of her body as his fiercely dark gaze pinned her down. There was a rage behind his eyes. Misha could feel those winter orbs sweeping over her whole body with immense displeasure.

Normally her first reaction would be immediate contrition. To feel an overwhelming sense of guilt for her actions, but the more she looked at him, the more she felt her own ire flare. How dare he. How dare he even try to get angry at her after his actions. He made his decision, the angry blonde staring daggers at her was his choice, so she needn't be concerned. Tilting her chin up she coolly turned her head and smiled at the chatty enforcer at her side.

"Misha!" the harsh sound of her name was easily heard over the thumping music. Instantly the guy she was speaking to backed off and disappeared. Steeling her nerves she carefully turned to Mikhail. His blue eyes were now literally ablaze with anger.

Slowly, partly due to the tall heels and fear, she walked over to stand in front of him and the infuriated blonde. Thankfully he was still seated on the sofa, making her feel just a little bit more in control as she towered over them.

"We need to talk." his sharp command an equally sharp gaze took away any feeling of control she might have had.

"Do you really think this is the time or place?" she asked, doing her best to sound aloof. Though she meant what she asked, the fact he was talking to her as if the blonde next to him didn't even exist.

"Time or place?! I am the fucking time and place. What is not the time or place is that fucking dress." he barked in return. At first glance, the laid back position he was sitting in portrayed a look of cool control, but the whitening knuckles in his tattooed fist signaled that he was holding back his anger.

Exasperated at how he could dare be angry with her and the random turn of the topic, she just shook her head and turned away.

Wrong decision.

She didn't even hear him get up, she only heard the blonde's startled gasp and the feeling of his powerful grip on her elbow. With no choice but to halt, Misha carefully turned to look up at the now standing mob boss. Despite her tall shoes, she still had to look up. Inches away from her he stared down at her with glittering blue eyes.

"You and I will talk tonight." his words were a whisper through set teeth, but she heard him loud and clear. Probably so did the men surrounding them, trying to witness the scene.

She wanted to argue, she wanted to hold her chin up and just walk away and let him figure it out. But it was something about the way he looked at her that caused her to just nod in agreement. The rage filled eyes held something else besides his displeasure, a look almost like the night in his bedroom. A desperate need.

The hand on her elbow lightly traveled up to her cheek, caressing it softly, in front of everyone before he stepped back allowing her to retreat. Misha didn't dare look back at him nor Krill. She just wanted to leave and deal with her pounding heart on her own. Meeting the stone-faced Leo at the stairwell she requested a stop at the bar before going back to her lounge.

What in the world just happened, she thought.

"What in the world just happened?!" Letisha's excited voice broke her out of her thoughts.

Turning Misha watched as Letisha squeezed herself in front of Leo, successfully shooing him away from the seat next to her forcing him to stand further away. Hopping onto the bar stool with such ease as if she wasn't wearing insanely tall heels, Letisha stared at her in rapture.

"Girl I was nearly hanging over the edge of the railing trying to see what was going on over there." Letisha was Misha's number one supporter when it came to her love for Mikhail. Though she tried to keep it secret Letisha claims she caught on to Misha's feelings long ago. Jay said the same thing, stating that Misha was so obvious.

"Nothing happened really, Mikhail just told me we have to talk later." Misha carefully sipped on the blue drink, Letisha borrowed the white dress she was wearing from an expensive designer Misha could not afford.

"Oh no, something happened," she bubbled loudly over the music. "He just touched you quite intimately in front of both his captains and a half a dozen of men. So something happened. Now tell me!"

"She is a whore that what she should tell you!" the area they were in turned silent at the sound of the shrieking insult.

Getting up from their stools both Misha and Letisha turned to see the blonde that was with Mikhail earlier.

"Excuse me?" Misha needed to clarify if she heard that straight.

"You heard me, your just a little slut trying to get in the away." Misha should have noticed the red drink in the woman's hands earlier as if in slow motion she watched the blonde flick her cup in her direction. With onlooking people on either side of her Misha had no room to exit the line of fire. Motionless she watched and felt the liquid coat her face and white dress.

The chaos broke out.

"No, the fuck you didn't." Letisha's angry yell was the last thing Misha heard before Letisha punched the blonde. Both women fell to the floor in a scrambling pile of heels and short dresses. Predictably the club crowd began to feed off the violent fight. Misha had no time to react, she felt herself being lifted over someone's shoulder and carried away. A brief moment of panic swept through her before she recognized the white designer jean-clad backside of Jay. His grip on the back of her thighs was painfully tight as he carried her swiftly through the now raging crowd.

"No Jay," she yelled desperate for him to put her down. "Letisha! Letisha is in that fight," she tried to turn in his arms, but he ignored her continuing in the direction of the back door. Frantically from her position over the crowd she tried to see Letisha. Thankfully she noticed the familiar faces of the bouncers breaking apart the crowd, and she caught a glimpse of Leo hoisting Letisha off the sprawled blonde. Misha wanted to cry when she saw the raw anger on her best friends face.

That was the last thing she saw before she felt Jay kick open the back door. Cold wind whipped up her bare legs when he stepped outside.

"Jay put me down dammit." she yelled.

"Sorry no can do," Misha could swear that Jay was smiling, judging by his voice. "I have been instructed in any situations like this, that you are my only priority."

"What the hell are you—oomph" he plopped her unceremoniously into the back of a black SUV.

"It's like a kind of training I have been doing with Mikhail." he informed her, as he jumped into the driver seat and gunned off.

"We can't just leave!" she yelled out. The ringing of Jay's phone cut her off, grabbing his phone while he maneuvered through traffic.

"Yes sir?" he answered, "Yes I got her...I'm taking her to the house now...yes sir...OK, I will tell her." disconnecting the line Jay tossed his phone into the empty passenger seat. Looking up in the reviewer he smiled widely at her. "No worries sweety, Mikhail told me to tell you Letisha is OK, and he got your purse and coat."

"Since when have you been training with Mikhail and why might I add?" she was yelling now, she didn't mean to but she was just so angry Misha couldn't help direct it towards Jay.

Pulling into the garage, Jay stopped the SUV near the elevator. "I will have to tell you about it another time, Misha. But I got to get back to the club and make sure our first client isn't confused or trampled on by the crowd."

Feeling a bit ashamed she forgot about Johnathan, she nodded before getting out. Waving goodbye, she went up the elevator. Walking through the door, she stopped to lean on the wall to take off the painful heels. Looking down she caught a glance at the damage to the dress. The red liquid now stained the once white cotton, pink ruining the entire piece. She could feel herself just about to give into her tears when she heard the door open and close.

"Misha," Mikhail's voice was behind her, taking a deep breath she turned to face him showing him the damage. "My God sweetheart I'm sorry."

Though his eyes held a rare glimmer of regret, her rising anger would not let her care.

"This is your fault." she accused him, hoping her voice stayed steady through her growing rage.

Eyes widening for a moment Mikhail stepped forward. "Ok, I understand you're angry..."

"No Mikhail I don't think you do." Now he was really taken aback, never before has she yelled at Mikhail. Not once has she ever talked back in any form, granted she never really had a reason to, but tonight she was so mad she was shaking. "This would never have had happened if you didn't bring your whore to my event."

Mikhail was momentarily stunned, his sweet little Misha was in a full rage—at him. When he heard what happened to Misha at the club, he almost had the bitch killed. However, Letisha's revenge was much more fitting, she all but destroyed the woman's face. After checking with Jay's on Misha's whereabouts, Mikhail made sure Letisha was taken to home.

Mikhail wasn't sure what he expected from Misha when he got home, but the raging ball of fire was not on his list of expectations. Doing his best to stay calm at her accusations he tried to think of something reasonable for a response. Despite the huge stain on the criminally small dress and the slight dampness in her massive curly hair, she looked gorgeous. Then he remembered his earlier anger when he watched her from across the club, flirting with that fucking singer.

"No this wouldn't have happened if you didn't wear that fucking dress." watching her reaction to his sentence made him regret every word of it.

"My dress," she yelled. "Are you insane, my dress has nothing to do with this. Furthermore how I dress has nothing to do with you." Misha realized she hit a nerve. The man before her seemed to grow larger as he stepped dangerously close to her, his blue eyes were like winter storms.

"Everything you put on, everything you take off, and everything you say or do Misha is all of my concern," he was right in front of her now. Refusing to relent at his overbearing tactic he used with his men, she lifted her head to stare at him directly in the eye.

"I don't see how?" she scoffed. "You already made is clear to me the other night you want nothing to do with me."

"Nothing to do with you!" he raged, "You don't know the lengths I have gone to, to keep my fucking hands off you Misha," he didn't wait for her to voice her confusion. "Besides that has nothing to do with this," he pointed out.

"Umm yes, it has everything to do with this. You just left me on your bed like an idiot. You will never know how much it hurt for you to walk away from me like that." she heard her voice crack as she quickly swiped away the tear forming in her eyes.

"I am not what you deserve or need. My God Misha, can't you see that? You have no idea the levels of sick and dark shit I get into. I willingly get into," he startled her as he cupped her face in both hands, allowing her to feel the radiating heat from his body while staring directly into the harsh blue eyes. "You don't need a man that lives his life on the outside of the law. You sure as fuck don't need someone who is ten years your senior Misha." his anger had a desperation to it. "Frankly sweetheart I shouldn't even be in your life."

"How can you say that to me?" by now she was crying she didn't give a damn about her pride anymore, hearing those words come from his mouth broke every bright emotion, destroyed every glimmer of hope and happiness.

Walking away in frustration he paced further into the living room before turning back around to her. "You deserve someone who...who is better dammit."

"I don't understand...do you...do you want me to try and find someone else."

"Of course the fuck I don't," he snapped, "I nearly had the little shit you were flirting with tied to an anchor."

"I wasn't flirting with Johnathan!"

"The hell you were," the look in his eyes told her she wasn't going to win that argument.

"I don't understand you say you want me to find someone else but then if I were to flirt with somebody you get angry. What do you want me to do Mikhail?" she yelled. "Do you just want me to sit around playing my little violin and pining away for you?"

A silent roiling fury seemed to radiate off his body, making Misha momentarily regret her choice of words. Giving her the iciest expression she has ever seen before he turned without saying a word he turned and left out the front door.

She didn't know her heart could break anymore, not once had she ever raised her voice to him much less argue. It made her sick to her stomach to even do so. But she had to stand up for herself on this, no matter how much it hurt. She was just so tired of being hurt. All she wanted was his love and if he wasn't willing to give it at least give her his blessing to find love. Closing her eyes, she wiped away the subsiding tears. This was the second time he walked out on her, he wasn't going to get a third opportunity.

Chapter 13

Sitting in Leo's living room, Misha absently stared at the masculine décor. The large olive green comfy sofa she was on went well with the beige walls and natural tones of the room. Though his furnishings were sparse, the room had an overall comfortable, masculine vibe. It was completely opposite of the white on gray she grew up around. Clenching her eyes closed Misha willed herself no to think about Mikhail and what she was doing. Leaning back on the sofa, Misha tried to relax.

"Here you go sweetheart," Leo walked out of the kitchen carrying two small glasses filled with brown liquid. Sitting on the coffee table in front of her, Leo handed her a glass. "This will calm your nerves a bit."

Though she never drank, Misha immediately took a sip of the strong liquid. Anything that would calm her racing mind at this moment was welcomed.

"So your plan was to take the violin internship offer in Japan and somehow not have to face Mikhail until you were out of the country. Despite the fact that the processing time could take months." Leo recapped her earlier plans.

"Yes I know," she sighed heavily before taking a healthier swallow of the burning liquid. The hot feeling from the liquid spread throughout her body making her feel warmer. "The plan was terrible. But I needed to leave Leo, and this morning I planned on just getting out for a little bit. But I found myself gathering an overnight bag, my violin, and passport. I realized the absurdity of my plan when I sat in the library waiting for you to come pick me up. I just don't know what to do anymore." she confessed, doing her best to hold back the tears of frustration.

"No sweetheart it's not absurd," he put down his glass beside him and moved to sit on the sofa next to her. "I am just glad you called me."

"I couldn't call anyone else, thank you so much Leo for letting me stay here." she smiled at him.

"Of course sweetheart," she felt his arm go around her shoulder pulling her closer to him. "You know I would do anything for you." Looking up she felt her heart jump a little, at the intensity in his gaze, she started to open her mouth to say something but he cut her off. "You know Misha, you and I can always leave this place."

"What?" she asked, confused at his words. "I don't understand."

"Well you said you wanted to leave him, and I am just saying," by now his eyes had a spark of excitement, that same spark of excitement he looked at her with in her room that time she was sick. "you and I could leave together."

No, was the first word that popped into her head. No, she didn't want to leave her family, and she didn't want to leave Mikhail either. This morning she wasn't even sure what she was thinking. She was just so hurt and angry with Mikhail, she just needed a breather.

"No Leo I..." the chirp of her phone interrupted her, looking down she felt her stomach drop at the text message.

'I know you are not at home, nor with your friends, or with Krill. Pick up your phone Misha.'

"Mikhail knows I am gone," she looked up to see Leo's eyes flash with anger. "I guess I should take him off of call block, or he will find me and it won't be good."

"Yeah I should probably turn my phone on before he has me killed," Leo's laugh was dry and laced with a touch of resentment as he walked to the kitchen counter to grab his phone. "But listen to me Misha, I am serious. I know we couldn't do it today sweetheart but another day. You and I could leave all this and start over somewhere else. Sweetheart, I would take care of you."

Misha had never seen the desperate look in Leo's eyes before. He seemed to be completely on board with the plan of them leaving. Without even looking at her phone she just smiled softly while turning off the call block, as he talked about the in and out workings of their escape. The moment she pressed OK, her phone rang. Misha was thankful for the interruption, Leo seemed to be very serious about 'their escape', and it honestly scared her a bit.

Quickly answering the phone, Mikhail's deep voice greeted her.

"Where the fuck are you?" His brusque tone gave Misha pause to regret, she wasn't sure which one was worst Leo's plans or Mikhail's rage.

"I am at Leo's." she whispered, waiting for his reaction.

"Then open the door before I break it down." the line went dead as she stared wide eyed at Leo's confused face.

Standing up shakily she grabbed her bag and violin, "Mikhail said to open the door."

Realization passed over Leo as he let out a curse before walking to his door. Opening the door, Leo barely had time to back away before Mikhail barged inside. The look on his face told Misha he was mere seconds from kicking down the door. With one look at her holding her things his face darkened.

"Come Misha." he said slowly through set teeth.

Quickly she followed him out and down the apartment stairs, only turning to wave at Leo before turning back to keep up with Mikhail's long angry strides. Sitting in the black Porsche, they rode in silence away from Leo's apartments. Misha could see by Mikhail's lethal grip on the steering wheel that it would be best if she didn't say anything.

Parking in his designated spot in the underground garage, Mikhail shut off the powerful engine. Misha felt her heart beat wildly in her chest as he sat unmoving, staring straight forward. The strong muscles in his jaw twitched violently.

"Don't you ever leave me again." though he didn't say it, his words held a dire consequence. Shoving his door open he got out of the car, quickly she grabbed her things and caught up with him waiting for her by the elevator. Stepping onto the enclosed space, she clutched her violin case protectively in front of her, anything to shield her from his raw anger. As if sensing what she was doing he snatched her case away from her, throwing it on the ground behind him.

"Mikhail!" she screamed as he shoved her against the elevator wall.

"Do you know what it felt like to come home and see that you have ran away from me?" he snarled at her, his face inches from hers. Though he only used a fraction of his weight to pin her to the wall, Misha could not budge. She always knew Mikhail was strong, but now she realized the depth of strength and just how helpless she was against his rage. But as she looked into his fiery eyes, she knew without a doubt he wouldn't hurt her.

"I am sorry Mikhail, but I just needed to get away." she tried to keep her voice calm.

"Away from me you mean." he ground out, wanting her to admit it.

"Yes, from you." she admitted somberly, feeling his grip on her shoulders flex.

"And you thought to run to Leo Maslak?" his whispered in betrayal. "Why Misha, do you love Maslak?"

"God no Mikhail," she protested, shocked he would even assume that. Pushing back a little, she was surprised to see him let her go, but he stayed in the same position unmoving until she finished. "I only love you, I am not sure how many times I have to tell you that. Though it does me no good."

"Misha." he warned, letting her know not to go down that route.

Finally the elevator dinged, letting them off on their floor. Grabbing her things as well as her elbow, he lightly dragged her into the living room, before tossing her things on the sofa. Frustrated she paced the living room as he stood like a mountain in the middle of the room, waiting for her to continue.

"I only called Leo because I didn't have anywhere else to go. Jay is supposedly training with you or something, I didn't want to involve Letisha in any more of my drama, and Krill would just send me back to you."

"Anywhere else to go?" he repeated disbelieving. "Misha, I have never given you a reason to run from me."

"Ha!" By now she was sick and tired of the back and forth, ignoring him she stepped around the couch to grab her things as she spoke. "Mikhail I don't even know what I am to you anymore."

"You're mine." Grabbing her arm he hauled her close to his hard, unyielding body, before wrapping his arms around her in a vice grip.

With wide eyes, she stared at his face shift from anger into a calm storm as if he came to some decision. Glacial blue eyes stared at her deeply while one hand smoothed back the hair that was in her face. Even through her jeans she could feel the heat of his body envelop her while she felt the strong, steady rhythm of his heart beneath her squished breast.

"Your mine Misha," he growled low, causing her whole body to stir. "Everything you are and everything you have to offer," his hand trailed down her neck, past her arm to settle on her waist possessively. "Belong to me."

"And you? Will I get to have you as well?" she whispered boldly.

Smiling a rare smile, he dipped his head to her throat and nipped at the soft skin. Holding back a cry of shock, Misha breathed deeply as he whispered in her ear.

"Soon my little Misha, just give me a little more time." with that, he stepped away and walked to his room.

With her body in a state of fever and very confused Misha slowly peeled herself from the wall. What just happened? What did he mean? Was he giving her a chance? Dammit, she wished she had concrete answers. As quickly as a blink she felt the familiar seedling of hope spring forward. Well in two weeks it will be her birthday. Is that what he meant by soon? If so, what did he plan to give her?

Chapter 14

He wasn't getting any work done. For the last two hours, the only thing Mikhail successfully accomplished was driving himself crazy. Staring absently out of his office window overlooking the shipyards he let his mind drift for the millionth time to his Misha.

Why in God's name was he so bewitched by her that it affected his control? Why did he tell her "soon" last night? And when did he become such a huge pedophile? God he should just cut whatever this was between them off. Nothing between them had really started, he still had time to end it.

Mikhail nearly laughed out loud, as if he could ever just walk away from her. Not to mention he has been obsessed with her for years but somehow, in some slow fiendish fashion Misha crept into his heart ingraining every aspect of her bright personality into his dark soul. It wasn't just her beautiful innocence that attracted him, it was her unwavering love. Hell her silent treatment towards him during their fight nearly killed him. It was then Mikhail realized that he needed her in a way that scared him.

Hell who was he kidding, Mikhail realized he needed her long before that.

Two years ago his usually solid discipline took another blow to the knees, allowing the forbidden emotions to take deeper root. Their relationship was just how it always was, he was reserved and mildly friendly while she was bold and outward in her affections. It worked great. Their days were consistent, just the way he liked it. Waking up and going to bed to Misha's sweet smile were his basic requirements for their relationship. While on the inside his dark fucked up mind could be left to wander. Yes, he was aware of her growing emotions towards him, but he was prepared to avoid the topic as long as possible. Besides in some perverse way, he liked subversively watching her affection for him grow. Things were perfect just the way they were.

Fate hated him.

As usual he was up before her, sitting on the bar stool he scanned through his emails as he waited for the familiar noise of her bedroom door. Within moments, she appeared though today was a little off. Wearing one of his pilfered shirts, which went past her knees, she slowly came shuffling out of her room in her yellow polka dot house slippers.

"Running a little behind?" he questioned as he watched her push back her tangled hair from her face.

"No school today," she half yawned as she poured two cups of coffee. Turning she finally looked directly at him, giving him a tired smile.

Sliding his phone back into his pocket he grabbed the offered mug. With her head propped in her hand, she tiredly drank her coffee on the stool across the kitchen island between them.

"Why aren't you dressed?" she asked as she stared at his plain t-shirt and sweat pants. Normally he would be dressed for work already.

"I actually don't have anything I need to be there for this morning," grabbing a banana from the fruit bowl he began to peel it. "Figured I get in a workout this morning or swim."

Her eyes seemed to light up at the mention of swimming. "That does sound good. Maybe I will finally redeem that Groupon I bought for a swim class." Grabbing her phone that was charging on the counter, she began to scroll through her emails.

For a moment, he actually had to process what she said a couple of times in his head before he could respond. "Misha, are you telling me, you don't know how to swim?"

Looking up from her phone she smiled innocently. "Yeah. I never really had a chance to learn."

What the hell was she talking about? Setting down the half eaten banana he gave her his full attention. "You have been here for six years now. In a building, that has an indoor pool. How the hell are you telling me you don't know how to swim? I thought Nico and Vera used to come over to swim with you."

Tilting her head as if trying to remember, she thought for a couple of moments before laughing softly. "Oh, we didn't actually swim. They just liked lounging in the hot tub, and so did I. I would stay in there until I got woozy, and then Nico would bring me back up."

That lying piece of shit, Nico always told him she got exhausted from swimming. Sitting back he just stared at her cheerful face for a moment before making a decision.

"Get your suit on." Eating the last of his fruit he walked towards his room.

Making sure the concierge closed off the pool, allowed them to have the Olympic size pool to themselves. Mikhail's wasn't surprised to see that just as in everything else Misha was a quick study. With ease, she picked up floating and a rudimentary version of the front crawl. However, what did initially surprise him was her suit. When she came out of her room to meet him by the elevator, she just wore a plain cotton cover up. It wasn't until they were poolside did he get to see what she was actually wearing. Stunned he watched her excitedly toss off her cover up the reveal a deep navy blue two piece. A part of him wanted to tell her to go get a less revealing suit, like a one piece or something.

However, the rational side of his brain admitted that in actuality the suit was pretty conservative for a two piece. The top reminded him of a sports bra while the matching bottoms were shorts, making it look rather sporty. Though no matter how "sporty" the suit was intended to look it didn't do a damn thing to hide his charge's developing assets. It wasn't easy purposely ignoring her growing beauty over the years, every time Mikhail slipped up and took note he regretted it. Now he was taking full notice of the heavy weight of her breast as she adjusted the straps to her top. The slight bounce to her round ass as she turned to position her towel on the lounger. All of this was just another reminder it was no longer just a kid he lived with but rather a young woman. After getting into the water, he was able to push the shock of the disturbing path his mind was taking.

Breathing heavily after coming off her lap she clutched onto the side of the pool and turned and looked at him with a large smile on her face. "Oh my God this is so much fun."

With a half smile he nodded. "You still have much to learn. Such as not clinging to the wall."

Her beautiful face scrunched in frustration.

With ease, he was able to tread water in the fifteen-foot deep pool, Misha—not so much. All the other lessons seem to come easily to her except this one. There was still fear in her eyes every time she went underneath the water. Swimming across the surface seemed to be fine, but swimming underneath the surface she freaked out. Panic would set in, and she would begin to sink. Every time he was right by her side to pull her upright, but it took some considerable coaxing on his part to get her to let go.

"You know I won't let anything happen to you?" He was serious. There was nothing he wouldn't do to keep her safe, happy, and by his side.

"Oh I know!" she exclaimed, "I know you wouldn't let me drown. It's just that it is all so overwhelming and kind of scary." Smiling she turned so that her back was facing the wall while both arms held the wall on either side. "And you make it look so beautiful and easy when you dive below and swim so gracefully."

He was never going to get used to her compliments. It was as if he wasn't a thief, a killer, and a gangster. No, to Misha he was everything. Looking at her wet hair cling to her smiling face, he let himself get lost in her brown eyes. So full of trust and love. It was still hard to get used to. No one loved him before Misha. No one cared about him like she did. He wasn't a meal ticket, the boss, someone who could do them a favor, he was simply the man that took her in when she needed someone most. Mikhail knew without a doubt if he were to lose his wealth and power Misha would be right at his side—smiling.

Wrapping a hand around her waist, he pulled her off the wall towards him. Instantly her hands grabbed onto his shoulders.

"I want you to see how easy it is to swim underwater. I want you to hold on to me, and don't let go." Her eyes were curious, but she nodded in complete trust. Turning so that she was behind him, clutched onto his shoulders. "Take a deep breath."

Sinking beneath the water, he pushed off from the wall with one leg and swam smoothly in an arch towards the bottom of the pool. Misha's grip tightened on his shoulders as he arched back up to the surface.

Mikhail barely got a breath in before he felt her come around from his back and hug him.

Laughing she pushed some of the loose hair from her braid out of her face. "Oh my God Mikhail that was amazing it was just like something I have seen on TV for Sea world."

"So now I am a whale?" he asked flatly. Leaning back against the wall he looked down at her smiling face inches from his, since she was still using his shoulders to buoy herself.

"No! You know what I mean, you were amazing, I just...I just wish it could..." she faded off, and so did her smile. Not wanting to look at him she averted her gaze.

More than a little confused. "Misha, what is it?"

"It's nothing really, I am just being..."

"Just tell me." He bit out.

"I just overheard some of the guys talking the other night at The Rose, and they mentioned you were," she paused as if to try an find the right words. "That you were dating someone. That you were dating the same woman so she must be special."

Mikhail whole body stiffened at her words. The workings of his sex life was not a subject he wanted her thinking about.

"And I started to wonder, one day you might want to get married and live with your wife, and I am pretty sure she or you for that matter would want me around to intrude." by now her breathing was getting a little choppy. "I mean I want you to be happy Mikhail but..."

He wanted to stop her and put her fears to rest, but it was something about the way she desperately clutched onto him with a despairing look in her eyes.

"But what..." he prodded.

"But it hurts,"one hand went to her heart, "it hurts so bad when I think of not being with you. I want you to be happy, but just the thought of not being with you anymore hurts so bad."

Her words went like blades through his soul. The hurting desperation in her large brown eyes made his whole body tighten in anger. Snaking an arm around her waist, he pressed her flat against his body. Mikhail could feel her heart beat wildly through her soft breast. Soft pink lips were inches from his while sweet brown eyes stared directly into his. The intensity set his whole body on fire.

"I am not going anywhere," he spoke each word evenly as he stared directly into her wide eyes. "and neither are you."

That was the first and only time he addressed his relationship status with Misha. His answer seemed to alleviate all of her fears but it only just started his. It seemed from that day forth an unnamed foreign emotion planted itself into his soul growing unbeknownst to Mikhail.

From that moment there seemed to be a connection he could never get with anyone else. It was wrong, and he knew it. No grown man should feel any sort of connection to a girl her age. But no matter how many women he put in his life or in his bed, the only one he thought about at the end of the day was the one person he shouldn't be thinking of.

But the mere thought of her in the arms of another made his vision blur in anger. The overpowering jealousy brought back memories of finding her hiding from him in Leo Maslak's apartment. That night he made a decision, he was done with Maslak. Thankfully Mikhail made earlier preparations to alleviate the problem that was Leo Maslak.

Bursting through his office door, Misha came and stood in front of his desk.

"Mikhail Kulakov what is going on?" Misha stood with one hand on her hip. After the kind of morning she had she forgot she was wearing probably the worst outfit in the world. Baggy jeans and a worn button down flannel, an overall very comfortable and non-alluring outfit. Pushing the Black puffy curls out of her face, she fixed Mikhail with an accusing stare.

"Do you mind explaining a little further?" he toyed with her, knowing full well what she was referring to.

"What happened to Leo and why is Jay, my new driver and guard?" It wasn't that she didn't love Jay but when she planned on having a girls lunch with Latisha it was a little annoying to have Jay happily intrude. There was no way in hell he was going to sit in the car like Leo either, nope he was right next to her laughing it up on her ruined girls lunch.

"I don't like Maslak, nor does Krill and I suspect—no make that I know," he got up from his chair and walked around his desk to stand in front of her while leaning casually on his desk. "that Maslak has some sort of infatuation with you. So I am getting rid of him."

"Getting rid of him?" she questioned, with a look of shock. "you don't mean..."

Laughing out loud Mikhail quickly answered her unfinished question. "Misha you have been reading too many thrillers. And more importantly you have me confused with Roman. I don't kill people just because they piss me off--anymore."

"Oh yeah, of course," she continued sheepishly. "But I did like Leo and I will miss him. I just wish you would have told me first. I was on my way to have lunch with Letisha and the next thing I know I am being told that Jay will be driving me around now."

"If you don't have feeling's for Maslak like you say, then having Jay drive you should not be a problem," he stated darkly.

Letting out a large sigh she threw her arms up in defeat. "Fine Mikhail, fine. If this will prove to you once and for all, I am not in love with Leo then do whatever you like."

He smirked at her rolling eyes. "Besides you love Jay. I had him working with my men for weeks, and he is more than capable to look after you."

Turning to go back to his seat she stopped him with a delicate cough. Looking back to her she took the opportunity to step forward cautiously.

"Mikhail," she started hesitantly, trying to word her question just right. "I was wondering if I could talk to you about something— important?" God she could feel herself floundering.

Courage Misha! Get some damn courage. All night she had been thinking about how to approach him with her question. Initially, she planned on asking him around dinner. Last night she planned it all out and now all of a sudden here she was speaking before her mind could catch up. Taking a deep breath, she looked up into the intense blue gaze. Like a predator, he easily sniffed out her apprehension. Like a wolf toying with his prey, he walked across the office to close and lock his office door before standing directly in front of her.

"Now," his voice rumbled deep into her core. "Tell me what it is that you want to talk about."

"Well since you said that," she paused nervously biting her lip, looking away from him to focus on something past his head. "that I belong to you and all."

A heat formed in the pit of her stomach at her own words. Somehow admitting that she was his, sent her blood rushing.

"Yes," he urged her to continue, his eyes lighting up with feral excitement.

Taking a noticeably deep breath, she timidly looked directly in his eyes and continued. "And you kind of suggested that we were going to be changing the status of our...of our...relationship, right?"

"I did," he growled stepping closer. His answer seemed to lighten some of the apprehension in her eyes and emboldened her to continue.

"Well, I was wondering if," she closed her eyes tightly before opening them back up and staring determinedly in his eyes. "if I could get an early birthday present?"

By now the tension in the room was so thick, it was clear this "early present" she was going to request would be unconventional.

"What is it that you want?" All Mikhail wanted to do was touch her, to soothe away the visible nervousness. He refrained however, he had a much more pressing desire, to see her ask him all on her own what exactly she wanted. By now his whole body was taught with anticipation at her next words.

For the longest there was nothing, she just stood there wringing her fingers staring at him absently. He could damn near see the war she was having with herself in her eyes. God, it was killing him, he hadn't felt this worked up in ages. Flexing the death grip he had on the desk behind him, Mikhail fought for control to be patient.

"I want you to kiss me." she finally blurted out.

Dear God words never sounded so sweet, it was exactly what he feared and hoped. He hoped that she would ask him for something like this, and then that one remaining sensible side of his mind feared it. Self-doubt raced back into his mind, doubt of his intentions towards her. But when he looked up to see the doubt creep into her eyes at his silence he made the decision.

Not giving her time to react he quickly grabbed her around the waist and pulled her flush against his body.

"I am only going to ask you this once Misha." watching her eyes go wide he continued. "And remember. "This will be your only opportunity to back out of this, do you understand me?" receiving a vigorous nod in reply. "Do you really want to spend the rest of your life with a man like me?"

A slow smile spread over her soft lips as a look of complete assurance washed away the last of her fears. "Mikhail I have been trying to get you to notice me since I was fifteen. I really think I should be the one asking you that question."

Grabbing a hand full of her hair he made her pay for that comment in the best way. Crushing his lips to hers, he drank in her cry of surprise. Delicate hands clutched at his shirt as he sought control over her lips. The kiss was carnal and filled with a needy desperation. At this point, his mind was a cloud of foggy desire, giving him hardly any faculties of control. Greedily he let his hands slide down her body until it reached her rounded ass. Spurred on my her moans in response he gripped the soft flesh in his hands. The extraordinary softness was everything he imagined they would be. Lifting her up he turned and switched their positions. The taste of her was exquisite, Mikhail could feel himself lose control. Moving his hands from her waist, he let the slide underneath her top to the warm, smooth skin beneath. Pulling away from her swollen lips, he looked into her hazy eyes as he slipped off the jacket and lifted the shirt, exposing her simple black bra. Groaning at the site of the soft globes of flesh demurely covered he leaned down to kiss the top of her breast. With a startled gasp, Misha clasped the back of his head in support as he showered her breast with attention. Just as his hand reached to yank the thin bra strap down a whisper of warning seeped into his thoughts.

"Wait." he commanded more to himself than to her.

"What! No Mikhail, I thoug..." He silenced her growing agitation with a quick, forceful kiss.

"Remember when I told you to never feel bad to go after what you want?" she nodded slowly with narrowed eyes as she tried to sit up straight. Seeing her trying to put her defenses back up he held her still with one hand while he gently ran his hand across the swell of her breast. Mikhail didn't miss the shudder that ran through her body. Steeling his resolve, he continued, despite the desire to rip off every article of clothing until she was naked on the desk.

"Well for the first time in years Misha I started to feel guilty about what I want the most. I tried to deny myself. But not anymore." he squeezed her tighter to him, watching her face light up with hope. "I know what I want, and I know what I am going to have."

"Oh yes Mikhail," her lips being boldly pressed against his nearly undid his tightly laced control. Growling in frustration, he pulled away and stepped back.

"But dammit Misha, I refuse to take it all until your eighteenth birthday. I am going to die knowing I wasn't a complete child predator."

Misha pouted at his professed commitment. "But I don't want to wait anymore, Mikhail."

"Jesus," he muttered to himself as he stepped away to fortify himself behind the safety of his desk. She might never know how her words just then went straight to his dick. Hearing her frustrated grumbles he watched, while thanking every God in existence, as she adjusted her clothes back. The state he was in physically and mentally anything could break his carefully built control.

Adjusting her last button, Mikhail watched a slow smile form on her beautiful face as she stepped closer to come around his desk.

"Stop," he held up his hand. He did his best to give her his most serious look, and not betray his fragile thread of will. With knowing amusement in her eyes, her smile grew larger as she leaned against one of the chairs in front of his desk.

"I think I have waited long enough Mikhail," her seductive smile sent tremors of need throughout his body. That smile should be registered as a weapon. "but I will we patient just for a little bit longer."

"Long enough?" he accused. He nearly laughed, the little vixen didn't know the meaning of waiting. Hell at this point his body was so hard he could cut glass. "Good God Misha give me this. Let me at least have this."

He watched one perfectly shaped eyebrow raise in response. "I still kinda think I should be the one asking for favors."

"Misha I am warning you."

"Fine fine I guess I will wait," she held up her hands in defeat. Grabbing her coat, she quickly slid it on and grabbed the door handle. Turning back looked at him with a mischievous smile. "But I won't make it easy for you."

Chapter 15

True to her word Misha made his life very uncomfortable, with Letisha's help Misha was able to make Mikhail feel the frustration she had to go through for so long just in a matter of days. At first, it was very hard, unlike some girls her age Misha never has much experience seducing a man. Hell, she wasn't even sure where to begin.

Just thinking about the countless women she has witnessed pass in and out of his life, bedroom to be accurate, made her pause to think. Would he get bored with her? Was she just a passing attraction. Didn't she read somewhere it was a proven fact that people were attracted to things they could not have? Was she that to Mikhail? A taboo enticement that piqued his interest, something that challenged his male nature to possess. The clenching feeling of her heart made her sit down for a moment.

Locked in the bathroom of her studio, Misha sat on the cold tiled floor and tried not to let the panic slip into her thoughts. No Mikhail wasn't like that. Every since she was younger he always put her first, whether it was a romantic sense of love or not, Misha knew he genuinely cared about her.

About a year before she graduated, Misha recalled the time just how much the hard edged mobster cared.

It was late when Misha stepped out of her room into the darkened hallway. Earlier she heard the sounds of Mikhail and his date come in and go to his room. After what seemed like hours of restlessly tossing and turning, no matter what she did she could not get comfortable enough to fall asleep. Finally, Misha shoved back the covers. Once she cleared the hallway, she was able to maneuver much easier by the moonlight streaming through the large windows. Wearing only one of her secretly confiscated shirts from Mikhail's laundry, she quietly padded to the fridge. Not that she needed to bother being quiet, the other side of the apartment was like a sealed vault. No one could hear in or out when it was closed off. Leaning forward on the counter she reached for a cup on the shelf above her.

"Thief."

The deep baritone voice caused her to whirl around in fright, dropping the cup in her hand. The loud sound of the plastic cup hitting the tile floor filled the still night air. Sitting on the other side of the bar, encased in darkness facing her with his back to the living room, Mikhail stared at her with unreadable eyes.

"Oh my God, you scared me!" frantically her heart began to race, nervously she clutched onto the counter behind her, anything to still her shaky hands.

The clinking of ice against the glass in his hand was his only response.

Silently the severe blue gaze crossed over her body, despite the darkness, settling on her legs. Her bare legs! Dear Lord, she forgot she was only wearing a shirt—his shirt at that. Now his comment made sense.

"I only take the ones you don't wear anymore." her timid defense sounded childish even as it left her mouth. Pulling the shirt down further she stepped closer to his counter to shield her undress.

He gave her one of his rare smiles, inwardly she sighed, he would never know what his smiles did to her. The large predatory grin always sent a shiver down her spine.

"One could agree that I don't wear them because I never get to keep them in my possession very long."

Wincing in guilt, she began to apologize. "I..."

"Keep the shirts," he cut her off. Standing up, he walked around the counter to stand in front of her. Stepping into the little bit of light the moonlit room offered she could see that he was wearing his expensive thousand thread count 'around the house manly pajama pants' and a wife beater. Taking another sip of the dark liquid in his glass, he looked down at her with mild interest. "Why are you up?"

At this point she felt somewhat crowded and exposed. Not once has she ever worn so little around him, and now he was only inches away.

"I couldn't sleep," she prayed her voice didn't sound as shaky as it did to her. "I just got up to get some water."

For a moment, he didn't answer he just stared down at her in silence. It took all her nerves to hold his powerful gaze and not run off or confess her love. Just looking at him made her heart pound so loudly she was sure he could hear it. Clenching her fist she swayed nervously on her feet as she waited for him to say or do anything.

"Come here," his deep voice was like a whisper as she felt his hand gently grasp her elbow and guide her back to the counter. In a trance of her own nervousness she watched him splash more of the brown liquid into his glass. "water won't help you sleep. Drink this until I say stop."

Not trusting herself she gently took the offered glass with both hands. Slowly she brought the cool rim of his glass to her lips. Still keeping her eyes on his, she drank the bitter liquid doing her best to keep from making a face at the strong taste. The spicy smelling liquid seemed to warm her whole body as it went down.

"Good," he took the glass and downed the rest of it. Without taking his eyes off of her, he set the glass down in the sink behind him. "Now my little Misha tell me why do you like stealing my shirts."

A hazy warm feeling seemed to spread not only throughout her body but through her mind as well. There was nothing she did not want to tell him. Although there was still some far away voice in the back of her mind warning her not to say too much.

"I have always liked you," seeing his eyebrow raise she quickly corrected herself. "your shirts!" dammit Misha get a hold of yourself. Don't make him regret giving you his drink. Though she had to admit she was starting to feel quite wobbly.

"You only like me because you feel indebted to me," he informed her matter-of-factly ignoring her failed correction. "You're just grateful to m..."

"No!" she put her finger to his lips. A small voice in the back of her hazy mind screamed at her for her actions, but she didn't care. Misha couldn't let him think that was the only reason why she loved him. Ignoring his shocked expression she continued.

"I don't just love you because you took me in," she took her finger away from his lips, incredibly soft lips she noticed. But the action wasn't as fast or as graceful as her normal movements. For some reason she just couldn't take her hand away from his beautiful stony face. Lightly she let her fingers brush from his lips to the tightly muscled jawline, scraping over the stubble. Looking into his eyes, Misha noticed that he seemed to be just as entranced by her actions as she was. The stark blue eyes held a warm intensity as he stared at her with curiosity.

"I love you for coming to visit me every morning when you didn't even know me, much less have to. I love you for making it a point to continue our morning talks. I love how you let me control the radio in your car, I love how protective you are, I love your rare but beautiful smile..."

"Misha stop." she could see the uncomfortable shock run through his eyes over her admission, but she didn't care.

"No, I love you and I want you to know why," her words seemed slightly slurred. She tried to shake off the overwhelming wave of fatigue, she needed to tell him, she needed him know how she felt. She didn't even realize how heavily she was leaning on his chest until she heard the strong heartbeat beneath her ear.

"Wha..."

"Time for you to go to sleep." his deep voice echoed loudly from the hard chest she was leaning on. Forming words seemed to get so difficult, she tried to tell him she was sorry, but only a whimper like mumble came out.

"Yes, yes I heard you. You love me," she felt the iron grip of his hand grip her shoulder before feeling her legs being swept up into his strong arms. Ignoring her small cry of alarm he cradled her high in his arms and carried her towards her room. Though her alcohol weakened, body was slightly sensory impaired she could still very much feel the hot warmth of his muscled arms beneath her bare legs. "Now it's time for you to sleep."

Like a dream she was sure she had before, Misha watched helplessly as Mikhail slowly lowered her limp body into her bed. But instead of kissing her and staying with her, like she has seen in movies, Mikhail simply gave her his hard unreadable gaze before flipping the sheets over her and turning away. The feeling of wanting to cry threatened to overtake her as she watched him step away. How could she make a fool of herself like that? Her memory started to fade, she could remember him leaving then the next thing she could recall was him turning back and looking at her in complete shock. A look that the stolid mobster never let grace his face. Misha couldn't remember what she said to make him make such a face. That night she fell asleep wishing he would for once say I love you back.

~~*

The chirp of her cell phone interrupted her reverie, looking down at her phone in her lap she read the text message.

"What are you doing?" it was from Mikhail, serious and to the point.

Chirp

"I can't see you." Thankfully there were no security cameras in the bathroom. Smiling she texted him back.

"I'm in the bathroom."

Chirp

"You have been in there for a long time. You ok?" She wondered how long he had been looking at his monitor.

"I'm sitting on the bathroom floor." she texted back.

Chirp

"Why? Are you OK?"

She couldn't help but laugh as her fingers tapped away furiously on her next text.

"Trying to get the angle right on my full nude body shot I want to send you." she quickly sent the text before she chickened out.

The feeling of excitement and a touch of cowardice filled her stomach as she laughed nervously. All week long she has been torturing him with picture texts. At first, they started off as innocent maybe even childish 'I love you' and 'thinking about you' texts. But after confessing to the ecstatic Letisha about her intentions her text defiantly went up a notch. Shots of her cleavage, shots in a provocative outfit, and shots of an ample view of her legs and so forth. All were sent two to three times a day.

Since he didn't reply back to her pictures, she was forced to wait for her reply when he got home. For the past few nights the moment he stepped off the elevator he sought her out. And it was glorious. The first night he found her in the music room organizing her sheet music. Taking her by surprise he kissed her for what seemed like an eternity, before pulling back and leaving her dazed out of her mind.

Last night was the worst and the best, that day it was the picture of her cleavage in her new dress. Making sure she was ready she waited for him in the living room on the couch watching TV. Dropping his briefcase he took three powerful strides before he was upon her. Misha lost herself in his strong embrace as his tongue warred with hers while his powerful hands gripped her ass. Just thinking about it made her whole body tingle in want. Mikhail had her flat against the couch pressing his hard body against hers, she could feel his arousal press against her thighs. But just as she moved her leg gently against the large bulge Mikhail tore himself away from her and stomped to his room slamming the connecting door shut.

Damn that man and his escapes.

The knock on the bathroom door startled her. Slowly she got up, wiping her palms on her jeans, she opened the door. Standing there, Mikhail gave her look of stern skepticism at her jeans and old flannel shirt.

"You disappointed?" she dared to ask, not able to keep the smile off her face.

"A little," he growled grabbing her by the waist and hauling her out into the empty studio flush against his unyielding body. "But I am glad you didn't tempt me like that my sweet. I do not think I could have controlled myself."

Threading both of his hands through her curly black hair, he tilted her lips to give her the softest kiss he has given her yet. Just as she felt the familiar tingling rush through her veins, Mikhail pulled away. Groaning she plopped down in the swivel chair at her sound board. Smiling Mikhail leaned casually, with one foot crossed over the other against the counter next to her chair.

"You can groan all you want," he chuckled deeply. "Your frustration is only a fraction of the hell you have been putting me through."

Smiling brightly in response, Misha felt better knowing, at least, her plan was working. That he was suffering just as she had been for years.

"So were you really going to take that picture?"

"Ha, I thought I wasn't supposed to be tempting you and here you are asking about it."

Silently he stared at her for a long moment before grabbing her hand and pulling her out of her chair guiding her to switch positions. With wide eyes she let him pull her down until he was easily cradling her in his lap.

"Your torture is working," he kissed her softly before whispering softly in her ear. "I think you owe me, at least, a small taste for my suffering.

Following his ice blue line of sight Misha's heart began to pound madly as he settled on her blouse. Still in a trance she slowly met back up to his hard gaze.

"Take off your shirt." his gravelly command washed over every nerve in her body. Shakily she began to unbutton the long sleeve flannel shirt. Since it was such a thick shirt, she only wore a bra underneath. Out of nowhere a wave of fear hit her as she began to part the shirt. Pausing she clutched the material close looking away from his intense gaze, she didn't want to see his disappointment at her childish reaction.

Grabbing her around the waist, Mikhail quickly lifted her to straddle his lap, allowing her legs to hang off the back of the chair. Surprised by the sudden change Misha was intensely aware of his strong hands gripping the top of her thighs. Still clutching the shirt together, she watched as a tiny smirk formed on his stoic face. Letting his hands slide to the cleft in each of her knees he pulled her close until their stomachs nearly touched. Misha's lip went dry when she felt the hard bulge pressing against her center. In that moment, her whole body seemed to become very aware of the large man beneath her.

"Open your shirt." he repeated his command.

Parting the material Misha watched in fascination as his eyes grew
dark with hunger. Sliding his hands up until he settled just
underneath her bra, Mikhail swiftly pushed the undergarment up
until her breast bounced free from their confines. Misha clenched the
fabric she was still holding tighter in nervousness. Though she
dreamed about it so many times, nothing prepared her for the
exposing feeling that washed over her as she sat on his lap shirtless.
Nor did she expect to see the savagely hungry look on his face
before he began to feast on her breast. The shock of his hot mouth
enveloping her hard nipple made her cry out. Clutching at the back
of his shaved head she felt her body catch fire as he sucked and
nibbled at the hard bud. Far back in the recess of her mind she could
vaguely hear her ragged moan mix with his hungry growls.

"My God you are everything I imagined you taste like." his words
vibrated deeply across her breast as he greedily and roughly palmed
her other breast. His rough hands sent waves of heat to her core,
without even realizing it she ground her hips against his needing
more. With a few mumbled curses Mikhail nipped at her sensitive
bud causing her to cry out.

"Enough." He yelled seemingly more to himself than to her, ripping
himself away Mikhail easily picked her up off his lap forcing her to
stand away. Still in a daze Misha managed to push her bra down as
she watched Mikhail lean forward with both elbows on his knees and
both hands on his forehead.

"This is your fault,"" he groaned. "You're killing me Misha. I am
going to be thinking about this all damn day."

At first, she wanted to yell at him for stopping, the frustration he put
her body through was highly unfair. However, the sight of this
feared criminal tortured at her feet made her feel better. Smiling she
stepped forward and cradled his head in her hands. Looking up at her
he gave a frustrated glare before letting his hands grab her ass
pulling her close while he buried his face into her stomach. Misha

smiled as she felt the muscles in his large shoulders relax as he continued to sit there.

"I can't honestly say that I feel bad for you, I rather like watching you suffer a bit," the harsh squeeze to her ass made her laugh a little before continuing. "I really was going to send you that photo though, but I got a text from Krill about having dinner tonight. I felt a little guilty I guess so I chickened out."

An impossible deep groan vibrated from her stomach all the way to her head and toes.

"Don't bring up Krill."

With wide eyes Misha hesitantly stepped away as Mikhail slowly stood up. The sexual frustration that blanketed his face moments ago was now replaced with real frustration. Deciding it might be worth taking whatever it was seating down Misha quickly sat in the abandoned chair.

"Why, What is it?" with his back turned to her she watched as he absently scratched at the stubble on his head.

"What do you mean 'what'? Misha, the man, thinks of himself your father and I haven't even begun to think about how I am going to tell him about this," he gestured between the two of them.

Hell, the last time he had a real conversation with Krill it ended with the older man storming out of his office. Krill made it very clear about his feelings towards his fight with Misha. Unfortunately, during that time Mikhail was so angry about Misha's silent treatment Krill was the last straw. That day he exploded towards his captain, he told Krill in no uncertain terms that he was sick of the whining, he had given the man everything he wanted so when it came to him and Misha he needed to stay out of it. Though his rage quieted the captain, it did nothing to the man's anger. It wasn't until recently, precisely when Misha started talking to him again did Krill start to act normal, slowly returning back to his jovial self.

"I have to go back," looking at his watch. "In twenty minutes I have a shipment coming in I need to be there for.

"OK well, I am sure everything will be fine with Krill, he is always understanding."

With a dry laugh, he stopped and stared at her. Wide eyed, hair a little messed up from their earlier activities, and smiling while sitting cross-legged on her chair. Ten years surrounded by the mafia and still so naïve.

"You seem to forget my sweet that we used to joke and call Krill "the friend." He had a way of always becoming best friends with his victims."

Not giving her chance to respond he left her with a look of shock.

Chapter 16

"Don't tell me you're surprised by this?" Abram did his best to take the laughter out of his voice as he approached his moody friend.

Krill was next to him leaning heavily against the one way office window that overlooked Vital. The office had the perfect bird's eye view of the entire club.

Currently, he was staring at the familiar figure dressed in an all white body suit. Abram had to admit, secretly, of course, Misha did look extremely good tonight. Probably another factor that wasn't helping Krill's mood.

"Of course I did. Hell Misha's infatuation for Mikhail was obvious from day one. I just—i guess I never expected him to..." He let his sentence trail off into a grunt of frustration.

"You never thought Mikhail would reciprocate?" Abram happily finished his thoughts as he moved to the nearby couch.

Slowly the older man turned and shot him a dangerous look. "Yes dammit! How can I ever be ok with the thought of my angel and him together." by now the older man completely lost the calm he was fighting to portray earlier, he was in a complete rage now.

Grabbing a drink off the bar cart next to him, he gave Krill a quizzical look. "Well as I said I'm not sure why you didn't see it coming. Her love for him, them living together, her maturing into a quite beautiful young wom..."

"Yes, yes that is my point. 'maturing'" he emphasized. "She is still a child."

"Well, he really isn't that old." Abram did his best to defend the young boss.

Letting out an indiscernible oath Krill began to pace at the window. Stopping he cast an angry glare over the club floor. Abram didn't have to move from the couch to see who was on the receiving end of that look. Sitting in his usual spot in the VIP section, Mikhail was attending another of Misha's song debut.

"Do you know that that boy came into my office," by now Krill was actually sputtering in anger. Abram just silently thanked God no one was in earshot. "and told me that he and Misha were progressing their relationship." Krill was not a small man, so his increasing anger combined with his endless pacing made the floor shake beneath them.

"My God the way he said it, the way he looked at me as if daring me to say something. I could have punched him right then and there."

"That would have been a very bad idea," Abram advised cooly.

"I don't give a shit." Krill sank into the couch with a defeated sigh. "I just wanted somebody different for her and not so soon. Someone more..."

"Someone not in the business?" Abram offered while eying the stressed man over his brandy glass.

"Yeah," Krill paused, "I mean I guess so."

"Did you ever consider the fact that if she found someone legit all the problems that would go along with it? Problems for her and us. Or worse she might be convinced to turn her back on you." Abram didn't need to add 'just like your daughter' the haunted look that passed over his eyes told Abram he got the picture.

At that he shot out of his seat, resuming his original forceful pacing. "My Misha would never." though his words held conviction, his paling face did not.

"Look maybe you should try and look at it my way." Sitting up Abram a grabbed a handful of pretzels off the bar cart next to him. "Misha loves him, she loves all of us, she works surprisingly well in our organization despite obvious differences. Mikhail is obsessed with her, whether he admits it or not. What more can a father ask for?" Abram mumbled as he lit the cigarette in his mouth. "The boss has means, connections, he can keep her safe, and she stays close to the family. Hell, I am not even sure why your so angry. The time she brought up the foreign internship it took us days to get you out of your depression, and she didn't even go."

With a lengthy sigh, Krill stopped pacing to stare out the one way window again. Automatically his eyes sought out Misha. As usual, his angel was a vision, tonight she was manning the DJ booth. Another one of the artist, she and her friends, were producing for just got done performing. Krill assumed she was probably going to run a few more songs since their DJ Spencer was still chatting comfortably at the bar. Squinting something caught his eye, leaning forward Krill tried to get a better look.

"Hey, pull up camera 1S, the DJ booth." the slight edge in his voice prompted Abram to slide quickly behind the managers desk to pull up the feed.

"Ok, I got it."

Both men silently stared at the screen. Misha was standing alone in the booth smiling and rocking to the music as she continuously adjusted her equipment. The booth was big enough for a couple of people, but she was standing alone while Jay stood at the bottom of the stairs. Though Jay prevented anyone from going up, he was standing next to a large speaker preventing him from noticing what they were noticing.

While it wasn't obvious at first glance, Misha was talking to somebody. The slight nod of her head, the occasional laugh, it was evident she was leaning back talking to someone. The only way that would be possible was if the emergency door behind her was open.

"Check the door," Krill growled.

"I already did. The damn thing is saying it's closed." Abram checked and rechecked the sensor.

"Fuck," Grabbing the gun he laid on the counter earlier, Krill slipped it into his back waistband before going to the door. "Radio Jay. I will let the boss know."

Taking the steps two at a time he got to the VIP landing in record time. The fact he was out of breath and most likely red in the face momentarily silenced the men standing and talking. Recognizing his unusual state Mikhail quickly got up from the couch and rushed towards him. Within in a few seconds, he updated the young boss. Though Krill did not have an option to tell Mikhail about the security breach, he kind of wished he hadn't. The look of controlled rage was unsettling, especially since Krill knew who Mikhail was going to direct it towards.

"Bring her up here, now."

After being hustled out of the DJ booth by Jay, who was being uncharacteristically quiet, she was led upstairs to Mikhail's loft. Judging by the quiet, serious faces staring at her she has been caught.

Stepping forward, Mikhail stopped directly in front of her. Like the loyal friend he was, Jay completely disappeared from her side the moment Mikhail stepped forward. Misha could practically feel the silent anger radiate from his body.

"Before you start, let me just ask you what in the world was I supposed to do?" she asked defensively holding her hands up as if to ward off the large angry man.

"Other than go against your word and stand there laughing and talking with the fuck?" His eyes narrowed into cold blue slits.

"Oh no wait a moment, I never broke my promise. What would you have had me do? Run screaming from the booth or try to get Jay to attack poor Leo."

"Poor Leo huh."

Ignoring him she continued.

"Besides he was only coming to tell me goodbye. That he was going back to Roman's camp. I didn't see any harm in just saying bye, Leo has been super nice to me, the least I could do is say bye ."

"Nice!" Nico, who was leaning on the railing behind her, laughed. "You must have truly forgotten your first encounter with Leo."

Trying not to roll her eyes she calmly folded her arms and turned to smile extra sweet at his interruption. "No, I have not forgotten Nico. I have chosen to forgive him a long time ago."

"Forgiveness! My God." Mikhail spat disgust, before taking a menacing step closer to her until he was only a breath away. Looking up Misha watched in no less fascination as the muscles in his powerful jaw twitched violently. "Misha I don't think you understand the situation. Leo was given an order to leave and report to Roman days ago. Roman has not seen him, nor could we locate him. His apartment has been cleared, and he has laid low. Then he has the balls to sneak in, disable the security system and get to you. Unfortunately, I have underestimated Leo because he is sending a very clear signal he won't be leaving quietly."

"My angel we are just now realizing how serious his obsession for you has become." Krill tried to step in to shield her from Mikhail's growing tide of anger.

"Oh," was all she could say. If she knew Leo was causing this much trouble, she would have never talked him. Now she just felt like an idiot. "What can I do make him go away?"

"You," Mikhail ushered her towards the exit stairs, "will be going home until we take care of this problem."

This time, Misha had a feeling his words meant exactly what they meant in her crime novels. Leo was not going to survive his next encounter with Mikhail or wished he hadn't at least. Though she didn't much appreciate being ordered to go home, she knew this was not the time to question Mikhail's authority.

Nodding she turned to follow Jay down the back exit stairs that led to the cars. Feeling the familiar rough grip on her elbow she was surprised to find herself being pulled back Mikhail. Pulling her close he turned around so that his back faced any prying eyes, shielding her against a nearby wall.

In a low gravely voice only for her ears, "Don' think you're off the hook so easily." his grip pulled her flush against his crisp black suit that did nothing to hide the strength of his tall figure. "I am going to make you suffer for your actions."

Swallowing she felt her lips go dry from his statement.

"Suffer?" she repeated carefully. With her heart pounding out of just a touch of fear she boldly sought clarification. "Good or bad suffering?"

The low rumble seemed to emanate from his chest while his eyes flashed with a fierce heat. For a moment, he just stared at her until he seemed to come to some internal decision. "Fuck waiting, go home I will be there shortly." abruptly he stepped back and turned back to the group.

"Take her home." he commanded to Jay and Michael, who were standing near the back exit.

Though she didn't plan on leaving so early, her all over nervousness made her completely forget her disappointment. Clutching on to the banister as she made her down to the alley, her mind raced with thoughts of Mikhail's last words. Oh my God, did this mean they were going to go much further tonight. Just the thought made her want to scream in excitement. The only thing that kept her from doing so was; One she was so nervous her knees felt week and two she could practically feel Jay's death glare on the back of her neck as she descended the narrow flight of stairs. Turning around, she tried to offer a meek smile.

"Don't look at me or talk to me," Jay grumbled.

"Wha..."

"I am going to get the car." the smile in Michael's voice was evident as he quickly went down the alley towards the back lot for the car.

"You know what you did." Though Jay kept his eyes on their surroundings, he did shoot her a dark glare. "Dammit, you made me look like an idiot on my second week on the job while you were laughing it up with your stalker."

Misha wanted to argue Leo was not a stalker. But she knew Jay well enough to know when he was laying down traps for an argument.

"I'm sorry," she was getting really tired of having to apologize so much lately. "I really didn't know it was this big of a deal."

A noncommittal grunt was all she received in reply. Mentally she sighed in relief as the car pulled up next to them, anything to break the tension between her and Jay. Arguing with him was the last thing on her mind. All she wanted to do was focus on Mikhail's last words. Once the car stopped, Jay stepped ahead of her to open the door.

The door was locked.

"What the fuck?" Jay's frustrated sigh made her squint in guilt knowing she was the catalyst to most of his current mood. Leaning to the side, he looked through the passenger side window to signal Michael. Jay's face went from confused to stone withing seconds.

"Misha move!" he stepped back in front of her, but it was too late. The back passenger door she was standing in front of burst open. Sitting in an odd crouch position, most likely from climbing from the front seat to the back, was Leo pointing a gun. Everything seemed to happen within seconds. The muffled sound of the bullet from the long barreled gun echoed as she watched Jay fall back against her body. The sudden weight of her best friend's body brought them both to the ground. The last thing she felt was the crushing weight of her friend and a sharp pain in the back of her head before everything went black.

Chapter 17

Misha felt like she was drifting. Her body felt like it was rocking back and forth. The gentle repetitive sway kept coaxing her back into a deep sleep, no matter how much the little voice in the back of her mind warned her otherwise. The inner war between sleep and staying awake seemed to wage within her for what seemed like forever.

You have to get up, she screamed in the back of her mind. With everything she could muster, Misha was able to crack an eyelid open. The scene wasn't too much different, she still to be surrounded by darkness. A flash of light zoomed by. What was that? Was that a street light?

Slowly. Very slowly, her other senses started to turn on. The feeling beneath her was soft but firm. Flexing her hands to feel for anything that would answer all the questions that were hazily swamping her brain, she groaned at the amount of pain the simple movement caused.

"It's ok my love we are almost there," the familiar voice caused more alarms to go off in her head. Through her blurry vision she saw a pale arm reach for her to soothe her affectionately on her thigh. The pale tattooed arm seemed to glow bright, like warning amidst the dark. That is when she realized it. She remembered what happened. Leo shot Jay.

Despite the pain and fog she began to try and move. Her boots immediately made contact with a wall. By now her groans must have grown louder.

"Take it easy back there sweety," Leo's disturbed voice came from in the front, "We are almost there."

Dear God she was in a car. The firm but still semi-soft surface she was on was the back seat. Panic swept over her instantly. What was he doing? Where were they going? What was he going to do to her? With everything she had in her she tried to sit up. It was then she realized her hands and feet were zip tied together.

"Misha." he called to her. Misha looked up to see his eyes in the reflection of the rear view mirror. The same eyes of the man she trusted and considered her friend were staring at her filled with a desperate unhinged desire. White hot fear lanced through her causing her to let out a scream. With renewed strength she began to kick at the back passenger side door .

"Dammit Misha please don't make me pull over."

Ignoring him she tried to hook her boot into the door handle. Misha rather fling herself out into the highway than be Leo's prisoner. Damn her for wearing the tall platformed stiletto boots. Inwardly she cried at how promising the night started off. Getting dressed up in her sexy outfit and then Mikhail's proposition. Just thinking of Mikhail made her want to break down crying.

Did he know she was missing? Did anyone know? And dear God poor Jay. Please don't let him be dead. That was all she could repeat in her head over and over again, as she kicked violently at the window of the car.

The sound of glass cracking signaled to her and unfortunately her captor she was making progress. Immediately the car seemed to swerve and then immediately stopped causing her body to lurch forward a little, almost onto the floor board.

Cursing in Russian Leo quickly opened his door to get out. Misha's heart froze as he ripped open the back door by her head. Beyond terrified she looked up to see Leo's angry face. But it was the bottle and cloth he had in his hand that made her start screaming.

"Fuck." he cursed as he quickly wet the cloth.

"No Leo don't please." she cried as he got closer.

"I'm sorry my sweet but I can't take the risk. Don't worry sweetheart its just a little to make you sleep." There was nothing she could do to fight him off. The pungent sweet smelling fabric covered her face. Holding her breath didn't last long. Sounds of her own struggling seemed to distort and sound for away. Black dots surrounded her vision until they completely took over her vision into black.

Chapter 18

"He would have gotten rid of her phone, probably even the car by now. And if I were the fuck I would have removed any jewelry, purse or anything else that might have a tracker." Abram said in a low voice.

Still covered in Jay's blood Mikhail stood dead still. He could tell his lack of response was making his men nervous. The amount of control Mikhail was using not to burn this whole fucking city down to find her was starting to fray at the edges, as he noticed his hands begin to shake. When he was alerted by his men that Misha was gone he was struck with an emotion, he hadn't felt since childhood. An emotion he thought was long since dead. Fear. His sweet, beautiful Misha was gone and straight into the hands of a lunatic. The only thing that quelled the unfamiliar emotion was his steadily building rage.

"Where is Roman?" he asked darkly, as he continued to stare unseeingly at the night's sky.

"Roman is..." the screeching of multiple tires interrupted Abram's response. Five or six black SUV s pulled up next to them. "That's him, sir, Roman is here."

Krill's response was to be expected. It was more of a breakdown than a response. Out of the corner of his eye, Mikhail could see Krill's pacing near the end of the alley where they found Jay's body. Though several of his men stood as a wall between them, Krill's deep voice was clearly heard across the alley despite the distance. The makeshift fortress didn't do much to deter him from his target. Mikhail ignored his name being thrown around with accusations and curses. He knew the man was beyond sane at the moment. Besides he had no time to go over argue and most likely physically fight Krill. Every moment wasted was another moment Misha was alone with that fuck. Looking back to the SUVs Mikhail watched as Roman quickly stepped out carrying a familiar case.

Silently and quickly Roman walked up to the car next to Mikhail using the trunk as a makeshift desk as he opened the briefcase. Inside the case was a computer that began to activate under Roman's commands.

"I will have her location in just a couple of seconds," Roman said without looking up from the screen.

"Get ready to move out!" Abram called out after quickly picking up on the game plan.

With each of his men running to the cars that left only him, Krill, Roman, and Abram standing in the wide alley as the cars lined up ready to gun off. With his blockade of men dispatched that left Krill free to come closer.

"I want to know what is going on Mikhail? I want to know how the fuck you plan on getting her back?!" Mikhail was quite familiar with Krill's intimidating techniques.

"Come on," Abram tried to block Krill's decent. "not right now."

"No dammit," Krill's voice was cold and deep, like the bottom of Arctic ocean. Feeling a little of his control slipping, Mikhail quickly turned and stepped towards the angry man. Using his full height against him, Mikhail stood face to face with the angry father.

"I am going to need you to calm down and trust me to find her."

Krill's eyes grew wide with incredulous rage, just as he opened opened his mouth to argue Roman's voice cut him off.

"I got her."

Shadows flickered across her eyes as she felt her captor lift her out of the car. Her mind was still fuzzy from what she could only assume was chloroform or something like it at least. The sweet nauseous smell still hung around making her want to vomit. Fear, however, took precedence keeping her stomach at bay.

Misha's heart felt as if it was going to collapse due to the constricting fear. She did her best to lay perfectly still as he carried her to wherever. With each one of his steps, she could faintly hear crunching. What was that sound? Why did that sound seem so familiar? Dear God, she was losing her mind. Why was she focusing on some stupid sound and not thinking about getting away? Vaguely she could feel warm air hit her cold skin as he carried her through the crunching ground. When the sounds seemed to mute and the crunching abruptly stopped, she could only assume she was being taken inside. The fear escalated again.

My God how could she have ever had trusted him? Doing her best not to start hyperventilating in case of alerting her captor. Feeling herself being awkwardly lowered she nearly gasped when she felt herself tumble onto what she could only assume was a bed. White hot panic laced through her heart causing her to involuntarily to jolt. The squeaking of her patent leather jumpsuit, an outfit she now wholeheartedly regretted picking, seemed like a siren in the night when she moved. Eyes still closed she said quietly in the awkward position on her side doing her best to calm down. Panic and hysterics would not help her now.

"Are you awake?" Leo's voice sliced through her concentration doing her best not to show any out outward visible signs that she was cognitive, she tried to will her body to relax. Thankfully at some point while she was asleep he removed her zip tie confinements. Maybe if he thought she was asleep, he would leave her alone.

"Misha, my love," his voice had a sickeningly thick air of sweet desperation to it. She could hear him step closer to her, making her insides freeze. The sudden dipping of the bed nearly made her jump.

"Please sweetheart, I know you're awake." by now his voice was right in front of her, slowly she opened her eyes. Quickly she assessed her surroundings. Unfortunately, she was right initially, she was laying on top of a bed. A bed with a bright orange sheets to match the dingy puke green walls. The room wasn't very large. It has two beds, an ancient tube TV with a foggy gray screen, she wasn't sure, but it looked as if it were sitting on a wood paneled refrigerator. There was a dark doorway off to the right that led into what she could only assume was the bathroom. But to the left of the room next to the window that allowed very little light through the orange bed sheet like curtains was the door.

Her only avenue for escape. Finally, after taking note of the door's locks, she slowly let her eyes settle on the man she once called friend.

"I am so sorry sweetheart, I didn't want to have to put you to sleep like that." While his tone was remorseful, his gaze whispered insanity. Dear God all she wanted to do was cry. Here she was inches away from a lunatic and who knows how far from Mikhail. No! She must bide her time, Mikhail was going to find her she just needed more time.

Not trusting herself to speak, she gave him a meager nod as she slowly tried to sit up. The movement was a mistake, she was instantly assaulted by a wave of nausea. "Oh my God," she covered her mouth to prevent from throwing up.

"Here use this," she felt herself being pulled to the side of the bed to where she could see a trash can being placed underneath her face. Not able to hold it back she vomited into the black can.

"It's ok sweetheart, it's just a little side effect to the stuff I used." Leo's words seemed to surround her as he held back her hair. "that's it let it all out."

Afterwards, she leaned back onto the creaky headboard. The awful orange and green motel room spun as she watched Leo remove the trash can.

"Everything from now on Misha will be much better, you will see," Leo assured her as he cautiously took a quick a peek out the window before returning to sit next to her on the edge of the bed handing her a bottled water.

"First we are going to go, to New York, I got a few contacts up there that will set up with the with papers and supplies we will need. And after that," he leaned closer to her in excitement while his hand brushed away some of her hair from her face. She resisted the urge to cringe away. "You and I will go to Paris and start a new life just like you wanted."

Though her head was spinning painfully, she tried to shake her head in protest. "No Leo I don't want..."

"Yes, dammit." Leo's anger exploded, grabbing both of her wrists he squeezed tightly as he leaned in inches away from her face. The bottle in her hand crackled loudly as she squeezed it nervously. With wide eyes she looked dead into the unhinged blue eyes of her captor.

"Yes Misha, you told me." his voice was deep with conviction. "You said that you wanted to escape and we talked about leaving that night you came running to me from that sick fuck."

Too afraid to contradict him when he was so close, Misha just continued to stare at him as he worked through his own logic.

"You and I belong together sweetheart. I know you feel it too. But I have to get you away from him first. That asshole was trying to keep you all to himself while he flaunted his whores in front of you and everyone." Still painfully gripping her wrist be brought then both to his lips. "I would never hurt you. You're the only thing I need. We belong together."

The chime from his phone across the room blessedly interrupted. Kissing her wrist, he released her and got up to check it.

With her heart pounding Misha tried to control her breathing. It felt as if her whole body was going to explode. Between her fear and the mind numbing dizziness she felt her hands shake. Mikhail where are you? She wasn't sure how much time has passed from her abduction, but she had to believe he was looking. He had to be. Mikhail promised her he would always find her no matter what. Wrapping her hands around her stomach, she remembered the day he made her that promise.

Chapter 19

It had only been a couple of weeks after the red haired lady had lied to her. Misha was in her least favorite class, math when she was called to the front office for a phone call. Confused she took the phone from the office lady, who also doubled as the school nurse.

"Hello." she answered cautiously.

"Misha it's me." Mikhail's familiar deep tone was on the other end.

"Hi..." she began to chirp happily.

"Do not say my name," Mikhail deep brusque tone cut her off effectively. "I am calling as Krill."

"Ok." she said nervously.

"Gather your things and meet me out front. I am pulling you out early today." His tone held no clues to go off of to judge his mood just deep and directly to the point as usual.

The line disconnected before she could reply. Quickly she handed the phone back to the nurse who was looking at her expectantly as if to find out more information.

"My...my dad," that felt really weird to say. "Says I need to leave early."

"Yes he told me you have a doctors appointment." she smiled tiredly, the kind of smile that was more of a job requirement than genuine.

Running back to her class she quickly gathered her bag and violin. All the while her heart pounded nervously. Was Mikhail angry at her, he sounded very serious. On one hand she was happy to see him but, on the other hand, she was very worried as to what was happening. She hated change, change usually meant something bad as far as she was concerned. Every since she came to live with Mikhail every day was exactly the same and God she loved it. Every morning she woke up looking forward to the wonderful routine of her day.

Seeing the familiar black SUV as the front curb, she hurried forward. Opening the back door, she was disappointed to find it empty. Confused she looked up to the front seat as she slowly climbed in.

"Hey, Misha." Nico's friendly eyes meet hers in the rear view.

"Hi Nico," she smiled, "I thought Mikhail was picking me up."

"The boss said he meet you at home," he reassured her. "I bet you're happy to get out of school."

Doing her best to ignore the worrying pit in her stomach she talked to Nico about school.

Waving goodbye to Nico, she took the elevator from the garage directly to her floor. Holding her case with both hands, she clutched it close, like a shield to whatever was waiting. The soft bing of the elevator dinged as the doors opened, standing in the middle of the small foyer to her front door was a very tall well dressed man.

With one hand in his pocket and the other holding a metal briefcase he turned in her direction. Gray eyes meet hers for a moment in shock before lighting up with some sort of odd humor. It wasn't so much the man's presence that made her bolt for the side door that lead to the stairs, it was the slow spreading smile that beamed her way. It was a predatory smile. A smile that knew more than you did. A large toothy grin that seemed to be laughing at you, never with you.

Misha heard him let out a curse as she ran down the stairs. Her case banged the railing as a she twisted down who knows how many flights. All she knew was that she had to get away from that man.

Something wasn't right about him. Bursting through the door to one of the floors she ran down the quiet hallway. The floor wasn't like Mikhail's floor. Instead, of the whole floor being one unit, this floor had multiple doors to different units. Finding a small alcove near the end of the hallway she tucked herself inside. Quietly she listened for other sounds besides her frantic heartbeat.

After a few minutes of silence the buzzing in her pocket startled her, it was the purple cell phone Krill gave her last week along with her own key to the condo. It was still on silent from school. Pulling it out she saw Mikhail's name appear on the screen. For a moment, she just watched it vibrate. She wasn't sure if she should even answer it. Why would he say he was going to pick her up then send Nico? Why did she have to leave school? More importantly, why was that creepy man at their door?

The moment it stopped it started up again. Taking a deep breath, she flipped the phone open she held it to her ear.

"Where are you?" this time she was positive he was angry.

"There was a man at your door." she said softly in her defense.

"I know, he got there earlier than expected." he said with a heavy sigh.

"Mikhail what's going on?" by now she couldn't stop the hitch in her voice she was on the verge of crying.

"Tell me where you are?" His voice calmed a little.

"I think I am on the tenth floor," she somehow felt, even more, nervous not sure what his reaction was going to be. She shouldn't have ran. Now Mikhail was really going to regret taking her in. Still huddled in her alcove she didn't even hear the elevator chime at the end of the hall, she just saw Mikhail stop in front of her. Standing up she looked fearfully up at him, to gauge his mood.

Giving her a small smirk he grabbed her case she was using as a shield.

"Under normal conditions running is an appropriate response to the man you meet."

Following him to the elevator, she was relieved to see he wasn't angry.

"I am sorry for running." she said in a low voice.

Leaning casually against the elevator wall he gave her an unreadable expression before sighing. "Don't apologize, I have been busy trying to keep this a secret I didn't think about Roman getting here before me."

The door slid open before she could reply. Peeking out nervously, she noticed the foyer was empty. Clutching her backpack straps in fortitude, she followed in Mikhail's shadow through the front door. Sitting on the bar stool at the kitchen counter was the tall creepy man.

"I can see why you want to do this," the creepy man laughed at Mikhail, "She is a runner."

"Only because of you," Mikhail responded matter-of-factly. Stepping away as her human cover Mikhail introduced her to the man. "Misha this is Roman."

Quickly her mind registered his name. This was the other boss in Boston. The dangerous one. With widening eyes she watched him step down from the stool and walked towards her. Stopping in front of her he grinned even wider as he extended his hand.

"My God I can see my reputation has now reached children." Though his words conveyed shock, he still smiled brightly.

Silently she offered her hand and watched as his long rough hand gently and politely shook hers.

"You shouldn't be proud of that," Mikhail stated deadpan as he eyed the other boss's interaction with Misha.

Never taking his eyes off Misha, Roman responded, "I am not going to lie, I kind kinda am."

"Let's just get on with this." Mikhail sat on the other side of the counter and motioned for her to join. "Isaac is bringing up the last few things now."

Putting her backpack down, she quickly climbed onto the bar stool next to Mikhail.

"Today Isaac, you remember Isaac right?" he paused his explanation.

"Yes he was the nice doctor I saw when I first got here," he was a nice soft spoken man, much nicer that the free clinic doctor her mom took her to that one time she had the flu.

"Well, I am going to have him do a small procedure today," Mikhail explained carefully while ignoring Roman's growing grin.

Between Roman's grin and Mikhail's unusual cautious tone, Misha felt as if she was missing something.

"Procedure?" she questioned.

"I am going to have him input a small tracking chip in you."

Silently both men waited for her reaction.

For a few moments, Misha let his words sink in. "You mean like the ones dogs get from their owners?"

Roman discreetly covered his mouth with his hand he was leaning on, to cover his grin but not before muttering, "Priceless."

With eyebrows furrowed in frustrated confusion Mikhail ignored Roman, "No not like that, this one is far more expensive and not to mention more effective. This device," he pointed to the metal container at the end of the counter. The same metal case Roman was carrying. "Will help me locate you if for some reason you are lost. Unlike the chip you're referring to, I don't have to wait for you to be found, I can just track you immediately."

"It's important we keep this a secret." Roman's eyes glittered with unknown amusement.

"Even from Krill?" she questioned.

"Yes," Mikhail's tone was very serious. "In order for this to be most effective you must not tell anyone."

"Yeah so that means only four of us will know about this little secret; you, me, Mikhail, and Isaac. So that means if the secret gets out we kill Isaac first." Roman said as Isaac walked in with his equipment bag just in time to hear the threat.

"Oh" she wanted to ask more questions but Isaac interrupted nervously.

"I will be ready in just a couple of moments sir," Isaac said, trying to ignore the threat to his life, before walking into the spare bedroom she used to practice her violin.

"I will be back." Mikhail grabbed the case and followed Isaac into the room, leaving her alone with Roman.

Hesitantly she looked up only to see he was staring directly at her making it very awkward.

"I am sorry I ran from you," not knowing what else to say.

"Don't worry about it." Leaning backward in his stool Roman looked around the apartment. "Christ, the kid is boring, this whole damn place is gray and white."

"You never been here before?" Misha asked politely, trying to gauge just how talkative the man was. Now that she was sitting in front of him she realized he wasn't as scary looking as she initially thought. It was more of his demeanor was off putting. He had short brown hair that looked really soft and his eyes were small and narrow giving him a very piercing stare. However, his serious eyes seemed to directly clash with his large joker like smile.

"I knew where he lived but was never invited in," he mused. "I don't think I would have been invited in if he didn't need me for the chip," he smiled mischievously.

"Are you two friends?" Misha didn't know too much about Mikhail's personal life so any information was valuable.

A deep laugh was his response to her question.

"I wouldn't necessarily say friends, more like coworkers forced to be civil to each other."

"Oh I see..." fiddling with loose string on her sleeve she thought about what he said. "Wait why did you call him a kid...if you don't mind me asking?" she added politely, she nearly forgot she was speaking to a man just as powerful as Mikhail, not just another soldier.

The predatory smile turned almost soft before responding. "You're so polite and not to mention cute, I think I am going to ask Mikhail if I can have you."

"No, you cannot," Mikhail answered as he walked back to the kitchen. "You ready?" he said looking at her.

Hopping down from the stool she made her way around the counter to follow him into the music room. The usually empty room was now filled with stainless steel medical supplies. Now changed into a pair of blue scrubs, doctor Isaac stood near the metal gurney holding some clothes.

"Hello Misha, could you please go and change into this." handing her the thin material.

Clutching the clothes she began to turn before stopping.

"May I ask if this is going to hurt?" she looked at Isaac, afraid to see any disappointment in Mikhail's eyes over her obvious fear.

"No, my dear you will be asleep though it will be a quick procedure Mikhail thought it would be best if we make it completely painless."

"Aw, you're so sweet Mikhail." Roman's tease rewarded him another dark glare.

Nodding she hurried off to get changed, her heart still thrumming warmly at the thought of Mikhail's concern. Dressed in the oversized pants and shirts which she was sure was hospital grade, Misha padded back into the room.

"Ok Misha just come over here and we will get started." Isaac stood on the other side of the tall metal gurney, already wearing blue gloves.

Walking past the two bosses, she noticed that Roman was actually a few inches taller that Mikhail. That made her remember her question earlier. Turning to Roman, "Oh, you never answered my question."

Stepping forward her surprised her by swooping her up and onto the cold metal gurney. "He is a kid because I am older. By about three years."

Wrinkling her brow, she smiled at Roman "That's not that old."

That only seemed to make his smile grow larger. "You both heard that right? Isaac, you're my witness."

"No, he is not." By this time Mikhail had shoved his way in front of Roman to stand beside her. "Isaac," his command didn't even need words, Isaac immediately got to work.

"Ok Misha, I am going to put you to sleep temporarily using the same gas you would get at the dentist office," he waited for her to nod before continuing. "After you are asleep I will anesthetize the area and insert this," he showed her a small microchip encased in silicone. "I will insert this in your lower right flank."

With a final nod, she laid down against the cool metal surface. "Ok here we go, it will be over before you know it," he began to lower the translucent green mask onto her face.

"Wait!" she panicked. Isaac's hand paused. "What if I don't wake up?"

"You will wake up." Mikhail looked back up the doctor, "won't she Isaac?" His tone held no room for discussion.

"Of course." Isaac's nervousness was audible.

"Ok," she could feel herself biting her lip in worry without thinking. "Because life is just starting to be good."

"I think I might cry." she could hear Roman's smiling voice from somewhere behind Mikhail's large form.

The muscles in Mikhail's in face twitched violently as he tried to maintain his patience, but he kept his eyes on her. "I will see you when you wake up."

With the green plastic mask over her nose, she breathed normally as instructed.

"Ok now count from ten." Misha could feel the light touch of Isaac's hand on her shoulder as he monitored her breathing.

"Ten," she couldn't help but wish it was Mikhail's hand on her shoulder instead of the doctors. At least, she would always be able to be near him. "Nine, eight, seven..." she could feel her voice fade away as sleep pulled her into it's arms.

"Why isn't she waking up Isaac?" Mikhail's voice slowly filtered into her dreams.

How long had she been asleep? Did they start already? Misha couldn't really feel anything. She couldn't even seem to open her eyes.

"She..sh..she just seems to be responding slowly" the doctor's voice stammered, his fear was audible. "Misha? Misha?" she could feel herself being shaken.

"What the fuck does that mean?" It was Mikhail's voice again, but he didn't sound right, his voice had a frenzied edge to it. "I am going to kill you."

She needed to wake up. She could hear yelling and things crashing all around her along with harsh voices.

With the greatest effort, she managed to open her eyelids. Slowly piercing light filtered through. Blurry images moved in and out of her line of sight. One blur got closer.

"Hey, there we go." A smiling voice said above her.

The scuffling seemed to stop. Blinking a couple more times she saw Roman leaning over her before he was pushed out of the way by Mikhail. She wasn't sure if she was still dreaming or not but Mikhail's face looked alarmed for the briefest second before settling into a fierce anger.

"Say something."

"Are we done?" she was so confused. What was going on? Isaac pulled her into the seated position on the metal table. Misha still wasn't sure if the procedure was over or not. She could not feel anything. She was almost tempted to check her side where the doctor pointed earlier, but Isaac began to talk.

"O..Ok, Misha just look straight ahead." He brought out his penlight to shine in her eyes. He asked her a bunch of questions about how she felt.

But she was focused on Mikhail. He was standing very still by the window with Roman. The other boss was leaning casually against the floor to ceiling window talking in a low tone while Mikhail stood like a mountain off to the side. He didn't look happy. She was trying to subtly hear what Roman was saying while still answer the doctor's questions, but she could only hear bits and pieces.

"Things are going to get worse for you, you do know that right?" despite his odd words Roman's tone was humorous. Misha was sure she was missing some important details for his statement to make sense.

Mikhail said nothing.

Mikhail did not seem like that, the tension in the room that already existed when she woke up intensified. In a matter of minutes, Roman and Isaac were shown the door. Isaac left most of his equipment, but he only seemed too happy to leave. It was just them again like it was every night. But that night was a little off. Mikhail was in a strange mood, he turned from the front door and walked towards his room.

"Now we are kind of like tied together aren't we?" she boldly asked. She wanted to know. She needed him to say that they were linked together forever.

He just stopped and just looked at her for the longest moment. "As I said before, if I need to I can find you."

"And you will come for me right?" she stressed.

He just stared at her, her heart dropped in that moment. He must have seen it on her face because he walked over to her, standing right in front of her. His large rough hand cupped her chin and tilted her head so that their eyes meet.

"I promise no matter where you are, I will find you."

Chapter 20

"Here in a few minutes we will head off." Leo took another look out of the orange plaid curtain before walking back towards the bed. "Then we will be that much closer to our new life together."

A chill went through her at his words. Misha wasn't dumb she knew he wanted to keep moving and he would rather move by night making it harder to track his movements. If they left that meant it would that much longer until Mikhail found her. Looking at Leo, she could practically see his confidence build with each passing minute no one arrived. He was getting comfortable, his usually large ego was starting to tell his brain that he was in the clear, that there was nothing to fear. The fact he left his gun on the TV let her know that. Resolving herself she made a decision, she wasn't going to make this easy for him.

"Ok sweetheart," he started with placating but firm tone. "You can either walk calmly to the car or I can tie you up and carry you. I don't want to have to do that," he sat on the bed next to her again. "But I will if you make me."

She didn't say anything, Misha just stared at the man she thought she knew for years.

"Though I must admit," his long pale hand fingers slowly gripped her leather covered knee. "You did feel perfect in my arms."

One by one she turned off every emotion. The fear, her disgust at his obvious intentions, her empathy she once felt for the man that never fit in with others. Everything. Misha felt her heart go cold as her body filled with a burning anger. Anger at his betrayal, anger at his perverse intentions and above all else anger for trying to destroy her beautiful life. A life she valued above all else.

"Leo," she heard herself whisper, it was as if she was watching herself from the outside.

"Yes?" he leaned in closer to her just as she wanted him to.

"I regret ever forgiving you." for a moment she watched in pure satisfaction as his ego took a direct hit, but she didn't bask in the small victory too long. With all the speed she could summon she kicked out with her tall heeled boots directly at his knee.

The howl of pain he emitted as he doubled over didn't stop her, rolling to the side of the bed she snatched the small wooden lamp on the nightstand. In a quick arc, she swung it around into the side of Leo's head. He grunted in pain and fell sideways, halfway landing on the ground and against the bed.

Though it was seconds, it felt like minutes when she looked down at him remembering what Krill once told her when he had her learn self-defense. "In a fight you get either two advantages. You can bring them down and run or you put them down permanently."

Misha knew Leo's physical capabilities well enough to know that he wouldn't stay down long. Would he go for the gun on the other side of the room? Most likely. So her running wouldn't get her very far.

"I am going to kill..." his words were deep filled with pain and anger as Leo fumbled against the bed to upright himself.

With her adrenaline still raging through her, she did the only thing she could do. She hit him again with the wooden lamp base, hitting yet again in the head this time near the back of his skull. By now she was nearly on top of him as he scrambled against her numerous blows. Leo tried to block her hits while trying to grab blindly at her hands. However, she had the advantage and quickly jabbed wildly in a hacking motion with the lamp, which had lost its shade at some point, using the sharper parts of the square base to jab painfully at his arms. Somewhere in the back of her mind, she could hear herself screaming as she hit him.

During her melee she wound up nearly straddling Leo to gain leverage with her hits. With a surge of strength, Leo yelled as twisted her off of him, slamming her body into the wall. As she scrambled to get back up, she felt Leo's boot connect hard into her stomach. All the air from her lungs seemed to be replaced with fire, vaguely through her pain she could feel Leo pin her to the floor. Misha could feel his rough hands wrap around her neck tightly.

"Why?!" he was yelling at her but his voice sounded so far away. Dumbly she clawed at his hands on her throat with no precision and no strength backing them. Black dots seemed to scatter throughout her vision as she watched his face contort in psychotic rage.

Suddenly a large blurry figure blocked her sight before the grip on her throat disappeared. Vaguely she felt the weight of Leo's body fall on her right leg before disappearing entirely from her senses. Each blink felt like slow motion as she felt her body being slid backward then lifted from the space on the floor between the bed and wall. Numbly she watched a large man and couple of others pile on top of Leo. His yells turned into screaming then there was nothing.

The pain in her neck was so great she could barely move it, all she could do was stare blankly ahead as familiar faces rushed past her while she was carried out of the motel room. The grip around her was strong and warm, but she couldn't seem to find the strength to turn and look up to who was carrying her out.

"I got you Misha." the voice sounded familiar. "I am going to give you to Isaac and my captain Demitri so you can get checked on while I go see if Mikhail left any pieces."

Feeling herself shift uncomfortably from one person to another, her head was shifted for her allowing her to see Roman look worriedly at her once more before running back into the room.

So the blurry figure tackling Leo was Mikhail. He found her. Looking up into the night sky past the worried faces hovering over her she closed her eyes.

Mikhail sat on his bed and watched her breath.

Two hours. Misha was missing for two hours. They tracked them to a city called Miller Falls. Rubbing his hand over his face, Mikhail closed his eyes as he remembered the sounds of her screams from outside the motel room. The sound haunted him. But it was nothing compared to the sight of Leo choking her on that floor. Mikhail lost himself. He couldn't remember what happened after he tackled the fuck. The last thing he remembered was Roman dragging him backwards from the body screaming into his ear not to kill the kid.

No, he would never kill Leo. Roman knew what he wanted and Mikhail was thankful that Roman pulled him off just in time. Leo would not get the luxury of death.

Wearing a white neck brace lying very still due to the medicated induced sleep, Misha looked very serene despite the night's events. Not too long before, his room was filled with people going in and out. Isaac had inspected and monitored her while Vera changed her and combed her hair. Others just hovered either by the door or out in the hall and living area. Krill was kept away from him, thanks to Roman. The man nearly lost it when he saw Misha's condition. Not that Mikhail could blame him but unfortunately since Krill didn't have Leo to take it out on Krill directed it towards the next best option—him.

Why shouldn't he? This was all his fault. Mikhail should have seen the signs of Leo's growing obsession sooner, he should have killed the man when he did finally suspect something. Shaking his head Mikhail closed his eyes, there were so many things he could have done to prevent this. Sensing the impending fight Roman ordered Krill to go cool off before coming back, giving Mikhail a few moments alone with Misha.

Luckily Misha's injuries were minor. Mikhail rode with her in his lap all the way back as Isaac looked her over. They were able to get her to wake up for a few moments to ask her questions. Isaac wanted her try and talk, to see if there was any vocal damage. Her answers were dry and short, Mikhail could easily see she was still out of it.

Just thinking about what that sick shit would have done if they arrived one minute later.

"I am so sorry my little Misha." he whispered.

Leaning over her he kissed her before leaving the room.

Chapter 21

Despite the long hot shower, Misha's neck still felt really stiff and sore. She was standing alone in Mikhail's large white bathroom. A bathroom she only been in a handful of times in her life, including the time when she was sick. Since she was still recovering in his bedroom, she took advantage of using the foreign facilities. She woke up a little while ago. The room was empty, but she knew it would not last long. It seemed like she had been sleeping forever. Every time she would open her eyes it would be either Dr. Isaac, Vera or Krill hovering over her always asking her how she felt. Misha couldn't remember when the last time she saw Mikhail. Was he mad at her? Where was he?

Leaning against the long sink counter she stared at her image slowly appear through the receding fog in the mirror. Even through the thick steam, she could see the dark bruises circling her neck like a dark collar. Black circles framed her eyes, eyes that seemed hollow even to her.

It was her fault.

Grabbing the fresh set of pajamas Vera laid out for her on the counter, Misha fought back tears as she slipped on the satin shirt ignoring the pants. Jay was dead because she didn't listen. Jay, who was just trying to do his job, was killed because of her thoughtlessness. Her best friend was dead. A powerful cry caught in her throat as she tried to suppress it. But she couldn't stop the strangled cry as she sank to her knees. She couldn't believe this was happening, she would give anything just to turn back time.

The knocking at the door barely registered until she heard Vera's voice. "Misha, Misha are you ok?"

Swallowing hard Misha opened her mouth to reply, but Vera impatience won.

"I am coming in," Vera announced as she opened the sliding pocket door and came in. As soon as Vera saw her sitting on the floor still clutching the counter above her she ran over.

"What's wrong? Is it your neck? Is it hurting?" She didn't wait for an answer immediately she yelled for Krill.

"No, it's not that." Misha rushed out trying to wipe away the tears, but everything just felt so trance like.

"Then why are you.."

"Misha darling what is it?" Krill's booming voice interrupted Vera. Stepping around Vera, he leaned down and scooped her up without warning, holding her in his massive arms as if she was nothing. Misha had barely any strength to protest and besides she knew it would be futile with Krill. Once he became worried, he was a one track person.

Once she was on the bed again, she sank slowly back into the pillows. Looking at the worried faces in front of her, Misha did her best to swallow the painful sob that threatened to come back up.

"I am not sure how long I have been here," she mumbled as she stared at the wall ahead. "But has anyone told Letisha?"

Krill's large black bushy eyebrows furrowed slightly as he shook his head. "No my sweet but I can if you like, I figured you would want to tell her yourself."

Now it was her turn to be confused. "No, I can't," her voice cracked a little. "I just can't. I know I probably should, but I just can't."

"Wait a minute." Vera interrupted giving her a questionable look as she dug in her purse at the foot of the bed. "You have only been asleep maybe eighteen or so hours since they found you. We haven't had a chance to really talk to you with the sedative Isaac gave you."

Krill's face was dubious for a moment before lighting up with understanding. "Ahh no my sweet Jay is fine."

"Let him tell it, he is not." Vera corrected him with a smirk as she tapped on her phone at lightening speed.

Their words didn't help the dreamlike state she already feeling. However, the look on Krill's face led her to believe he was being sincere.

"Here we are." Vera came closer sidestepping Krill to sit on the space nearest to Misha on the bed. Handing her the phone Misha watched the screen as it rang. The icon for Nico disappeared and was replaced with his face on the video call.

His face looked scruffy as if he missed his morning shave, but his trademark smile flashed at her once he recognized her.

"Hey Misha, how you feeling?" the concern in his eyes and voice made her want to cry for some reason.

But the voice she heard next did make her cry.

"Is that Misha?!" Jay's deep voice called out from the background. "Tell her I am going to make her my slave for this."

"Here you just tell her yourself" The images blurred around the white hospital room as Nico walked over to Jay.

Within seconds she could see Jay's face clearly. He looked tired. Though he was grinning largely, as usual, Misha knew him well enough to see he was exhausted.

"Oh my God Jay I am so sorry." she couldn't help but cry all over again as she caught glimpses of the bandages on his shoulder.

"Ahh don't cry if you do I am gonna cry." he laughed.

Pausing she trying to control the tears another thought popped up.

"Oh my God, where is Michael?" she looked at the phone in her hand then up to Vera in alarm.

"I was wondering if you would even think of me." Michael's deeply accented voice drifted from the phone in her hand.

Jay rolled his eyes before turning the phone, allowing her to see Michael sitting on the side of the other bed. Michael was still in his suit from last night, looking as if he was just visiting.

Seeing the confusion on her face he smiled. "That little shit knocked me out."

"Yeah whereas I got shot!" Jay interrupted swinging the phone back to himself, "I told you he didn't like me. But that's fine 'cause I didn't like that piece of shit either. God, I hope Mikhail killed him slowly."

After talking to Jay for a couple more moments, and pledging her lifelong servitude, Krill told her to get some sleep.

Alone in the dark room she stared at the digital clock on the nightstand. It was eight thirty. The sky was unusually bright tonight. It wasn't its normal black, it was a grayish blue that seemed to hold just enough light to see clearly into the night.

Ever since she woke up, Misha had been ignoring the memories of the incident. Each time she recalled his psychotic face over her she quickly suppressed it. Never before had she felt so weak. The shame she felt for all the trouble she caused made her lungs constrict. All she ever wanted to do was not be a nuisance to the people around her, and in the span of a few hours she caused an uproar.

With no tears left to cry she let her eyes close as she stared at the bright green digital numbers.

Chapter 22

A familiar radiating heat woke her up from her plagued dreams.
Dreams of Leo's face above her as he tried to strangle away her life.
Opening her eyes she noticed the time on the clock, it four in the
morning. Though she didn't need the clock to tell her it was that late,
the room was so dark even the large open window did nothing to
break the onslaught of the dark. Turning in the soft plush covers to
investigate the heat that woke her up, her eyes widened when she
came face to face with Mikhail. He was awake. For a long moment
winter blue eyes stared directly into hers before she broke the
silence.

"I thought you were mad at me," she whispered not taking her eyes
off his. "I haven't seen you all day."

Ever so slightly she watched his eyebrow furrow in confusion
before he gave her his rare smirk.

"You have been asleep all day," he said in a low rumbling voice.
Adjusting himself against the pillows he sat slightly higher, against
the headboard, causing her to look up. "I came to check on you quite
a few times throughout the day, and I have been here next to you
ever since I got home.

Her lips formed a silent "oh." Not able to look into his hard,
unyielding gaze anymore she looked down though her neck brace
hampered her movements. She felt as if she was going to cry again.
Hell, she wanted to cry. Things just kept going wrong. Misha didn't
want her next time in this bed to be a pity party. The rustling of the
covers made her look back up. With a gentle strength, he pulled her
up until she was leaning against him wrapped in his strong arms.
Misha's whole body heated in a thrumming excitement at his sudden
affection. This was all she ever dreamed of.

With her face inches from his, Misha tried to advert her gaze from
his intense one. It felt like he was looking right through her. Her

eyes drifted down the strong cheekbones, past the lips that plagued her dreams, down to the strong column of his neck. Without thinking she leaned in to bury her face in the crevice of his neck and shoulder. Immediately her senses were assaulted making her heart beat wildly. Ever since she was younger, she has wanted to do this. To initiate contact and not be rejected. She inhaled his clean, crisp scent as she felt his strong arms wrap her close. The intimate feeling was almost too much, tears stung and threatened to form, but she just buried deeper into his hot skin.

"I am sorry Misha," his voice rumbled shaking her whole body in this position.

She wanted to shake her head and tell him not to be sorry, but the pain in her neck halted her actions. All she could do was shut her eyes and bury herself deeper into his beautiful warmth. Her whole body radiated in awareness of him. The large, powerful biceps that cradled her against him while his equally powerful thighs pressed against her buttocks, warming her whole body. Misha felt small but didn't at all feel helpless. Every inch of his strength was used to care for her. Thinking back to her earlier thoughts in the bathroom, she carefully turned her head from his hot chest to speak.

"I thought you were mad at me." she whispered hesitant to share her earlier insecurities.

The powerful grip around her tightened gently. "Mad?" he paused as if to think about his next words. "Yes, yes I was mad. Hell, I was beyond my sanity mad but not at you, never at you." Shifting his arm around her, Misha felt her body lean backwards until he had her looking directly up at him in his arms. "I swear to God Misha I thought I had lost you...it..it would have destroyed me."

The intensity in his blue eyes made tears well up in her eyes. Using her free hand, she quickly wiped away the rolling tears. "I am right here Mikhail, I will never leave you."

His expression was like granite as his blue eyes searched hers as if he was coming to some sort of decision.

"I will hold you to that promise." he rumbled deeply.

Leaning over her he captured her lips with his. Mikhail held her in a way she could do nothing but take his advances. As she lay captured in his arms his hot mouth moved hungrily against hers, she gasped at the hard need in his kiss. Mikhail took advantage of her shock, giving him the opportunity to deepen the kiss further. Her hand that was caught against his hard body clutched at his shirt desperately as her breath was taken away. His strong arm anchored her head perfectly for his assault allowing his to take full advantage without her having to strain her neck. The tingling between her legs caused her to shift in anticipation while she grew bolder and answered his probing kiss with her tongue. His deep groan at her actions vibrated across her breast and down to her core.

Shifting again in the discomfort of her arousal Misha could feel his hard length against her soft buttocks. The shifting against him ripped him from her lips. Dazed and a little dizzy from the overwhelming intensity Misha looked up, and her breath caught. The rough need in his face took away what remained of her breath.

"We need to stop." his words seemed very contradictory as she watched with wide eyes as he ripped the button down shirt she was wearing open, ignoring the flying buttons. "You need to rest." It was as if he was speaking from a different place, the logical, sensible side of his mind, but the rest of him did not pay his words heed. His eyes lit up with fierce hunger as her breast were bared for him. Shifting her back further in his hold, arching her slightly until her breast were standing high ready to be devoured. And he did devour them. She let out a shriek as he nipped at her sensitive nipple. She wasn't prepared for the pain laced with white hot pleasure. This was so different from the last time in her studio. He was rough and completely in control. Her moans only seemed to spur him on has he violently sucked the dark bud in his mouth. By now her most private place was on fire with ignored tension. But Mikhail seemed to read her need, still pinching as rolling her nipple she felt his other hand move her panties to the side.

Though her body craved attention there, her mind still registered the sudden invasion at her most private area. Without even thinking her body tensed all over has he let a finger glide past her wet curls. Releasing her sore nipple from his mouth, he looked back into her eyes and smiled. It was a primal provoking smile that filled her with an unknown fear.

When she opened her mouth to tell him to wait, he sealed her words in her throat with his lips and in the same moment inserted a thick finger into her tight passage. Her breath immediately hitched has her body tensed to his invasion. He mumbled a curse against her lips.

"Jesus," he growled, "you're so small." That didn't stop him from pushing the digit further in.

She groaned at the feeling, a feeling that hurt a little at first but with every pump felt intoxicatingly better.

"That's it, baby," he whispered hoarsely against her lips as he slipped in another finger. "God how I have dreamed of this."

Now he had three of his large fingers stretching her impossibly far. Misha's grunts turned to screams as he went back to torturing her breast and stretching her pussy. The once tiny tremors that racked her body were building and building to impossible heights. Far beyond the feeling she ever gave herself. It was so intense it almost hurt, the building feeling was driving her crazy. Absently she could hear herself beg him to stop, he simply just speed up the pace. Using his thumb she felt him rub the small nubbin at her center, the feeling caused her world to shatter.

Opening her eyes again, she realized she must have passed out a little. She was now laying in the bed alone. Panic set in. What happened? With hardly any strength she managed to push herself up onto one elbow. The light beneath the bathroom door shined brightly in the darkness. Minutes later Mikhail stepped out wearing only some briefs. With the bathroom light switched off she wasn't able to see much. All she could feel was the bed dip with his weight. The nervousness washed out of her as he felt his arm snake around her pulling her into his body.

He said nothing.

Since she was facing the opposite direction, she could not see his face. But her ass was pressed against him she couldn't feel his hardness like before.

Self-conscious doubt filled her. What happened? Did she do something wrong?

"Mikhail?" she whispered, her voice was little hoarse.

"Mmmmm," he seemed tired. For some reason that only made her feel worse. Was he tired of her already?

"I..I don't understand? Are we not gonna..." she was so nervous she could barely get it out.

"Not going to what?" though his voice was rough from fatigue she could still hear the teasing smile.

"You know what I mean!" she was getting frustrated.

Pulling her tighter against him she felt his face bury into her hair. "Are we gonna fuck?"

"Yes." she stammered nervously. Shocked by his course language in this intimate moment, but a little turned on.

"By this time tomorrow," his hand that was around her waist traveled back up to her bare breast cupping it gently. "I will be buried deep inside of you." His words caused her breath to stop. "But for tonight I want you to rest because tomorrow I won't hold back no matter how many times you pass out."

She wasn't sure why that made her fearful and aroused. But she did feel relief that everything was fine. Boldly she covered his hand that was on her breast with hers.

"I love you." She whispered.

The deep groan in the back of her hair startled her. "Go to sleep Misha before you destroy my willpower."

She smiled.

Chapter 23

The chirping of her phone stirred Misha out of her blissful sleep. Last night was probably the best night of her life, including the best sleep. Instantly the memories of what they did or what Mikhail did to her flooded back. The thought alone made her body grow hot again. Squinting at the bright sunlight Misha turned her head to Mikhail's spot in the bed. It was empty. But this did not alarm her. Judging by the bright sun, she figured it was mid morning if not afternoon and shipyard business was an early business.

Reaching for her phone on the nightstand Misha answered the constant chirping. The frantic voice of her agent answered.

"Misha! Thank God I got you to answer," he was breathless with audible relief. "Krill told me that you were sick but please tell me you remembered the New York performance for tonight?"

Shit, she totally forgot about that. Tonight she was to perform a duet of course with one of the world's leading ballet dancer, Yuri Gusev. Misha was drawn to this performance not only for the direction of the piece, and that he happened to be Russian, but the fact that they considered her a worthy enough player to perform on stage with this legend. Ignoring her achy neck she jumped out of bed and all but ran down the hall to her room.

"Yes, I mean no," she stumbled over her words. "I did not forget I will be ready within the hour. I just need to call someone to take me to the airport."

"I have emailed your ticket, and I have called Nico since for some reason I can't get a hold of your father. Nico says he is on his way to pick you up." Her agent's tone was direct and efficient. Just like his management style. She smiled at the thought of her uptight agent desperate enough to call Nico.

Disconnecting the line she started grabbing clothes, shoes, and toiletries all the while trying to call Krill. Giving up after the third call Misha glanced at the clock, just as the front door opened.

"Misha Misha," Nico's smiling voice came closer as he walked down the hallway to stand in her room door. "You almost ready? Plane leaves in an hour and a half, and your rehearsal starts in three hours."

"Yes I am I just got to grab my dress bag and I will be done," she said as she ran back to her closet. "I have tried calling Krill and Mikhail but neither one is answering," she yelled from the closet.

"Yeah I think they are in some sort of meeting." Nico leaned nonchalantly on her door, holding her violin case.

Grabbing her duffel and dress bag, she followed the tall enforcer out of the apartment and onto the elevator. "Well they all have this in their calendars, I made sure of it. So I guess when they check their voicemail they will remember."

Climbing into the passenger seat of Nico's SUV he gave her a sarcastic smirk as he pulled off.

"What?" she questioned.

"Like you didn't forget."

"Hey I was nearly choked to death," she pointed dramatically at her neck brace.

"I was wondering when you would start milking that." Nico laughed at her pouty face.

Mikhail stood at the edge of the east dock; this was the storage area for all the shipping containers. Rows and rows of hundreds of blue, yellow, and red freight containers. Looking out at the calm sea Mikhail heard familiar footsteps. Turning he looked at Krill walking from an aisle of containers. Krill was out of breath and sweaty while his blue shirt has spurts of dark red spots. The men just briefly exchanged glances at one another as Krill kept walking back toward the main building.

The older man was still upset at him. Mikhail completely understood why, he just didn't give a shit. Krill was going to have to get over it. Misha was completely his now. Walking down the same aisle, Krill came from Mikhail approached the designated red shipping container. Unlocking the large industrial padlock Mikhail walked into the dark container.

A whimpering like moan echoed within the metal walls, as Mikhail turned on the battery powered light. Lighting up the darkness Mikhail looked at the bloody and broken man on the floor.

"Hello Leo," he said calmly as he pulled the available folding chair out and sat down. "I see that Krill didn't leave much for me," taking in the amount of blood.

Leo gurgled something that sounded like a plea.

Mikhail only blinked, as he watched the young man writhe in the fetal position. Leo was still wearing the black slacks and white shirt from the night he was caught. Though the shirt was completely blood soaked now. Mikhail hoped Leo liked those clothes because they would be the last pair he will ever wear.

"Krill wants this to last for at least a couple of months," Mikhail leaned forward with his elbows on both knees cradling his chin on his laced fingers. "But I have six other containers like this with my boss Vladamir's enemies and a few of Roman's too. I am pretty skilled at this; I have had years of practice. I can make this last for years if need be."

The injured man released a sad high pitch whining cry in response.

"Since you were so obsessed with Misha I figured I would give you an update on her progress." Mikhail smiled at the thought of her. "I left her in a deep sleep that I had a hand in creating," he smiled at the memory. "Last night I watched her cum in my arms, and I have to say it was far beyond what I expected."

Leo shifted uncomfortably at his words. Or at the wounds. Mikhail wasn't sure but continued nonetheless.

"Tonight the moment I get home I am going to spread her legs and bury my face in her sweet wet pussy." His body was getting hard just thinking about it. "God you have no idea how long I have been wanting to do that. And after she is completely fucking spent I am going to fill her completely, I am going to make sure she will be carrying my child by next month." Mikhail closed his eyes at the satisfied thought. He was getting excited, too excited.

"So you're in luck. Krill will be your only visitor today. I will see you again soon." Ignoring the man's crying Mikhail walked out of the container. Mikhail needed to get home, years of torturing himself keeping his distance from his innocent ward was over.

The day felt absurdly long. It didn't even feel like the same day as a matter of fact. Misha had to remind herself it was indeed the all still the same day. She woke up in Mikhail's bed, and her agent called her, she got on a plane, and rehearsed for seemingly hours, and she performed.

But it was all worth it. The performance with Yuri could not have gone off any better if she tried. Yuri danced powerfully to the music. The premise of the piece was that the dancer was supposed to be overjoyed and enraptured by her music. There were moments he was so close she could feel the whoosh of air from his kicks. When it was over, she nearly clapped herself at his dance, but she bowed respectfully to the overwhelming applause. After spending a couple of hours shaking hands with nearly everyone at the after party, she finally got to leave.

Sitting in the passenger seat of the rented car she tried her best to keep from falling asleep. Nico easily maneuvered through the New York late night traffic as she stared out the window. This was her second time in New York, the first was on a trip with her school for some national competition. Leaning against the cool window, she could remember herself doing the exact same thing in the school van looking up at the impossibly tall buildings. She had wished that one day she would be able to see her own name on the performance program. Now here she was completing that very dream. Excitement bubbled within her, she wanted to call Mikhail to celebrate about the performance. But she forgot her phone charger, and her phone was very much dead.

"Ok, we are here." Nico slowed the sleek black sedan to a stop under the hotel's large carport.

Grabbing her violin case herself, Misha let the hotel porter take the rest of her and Nico's luggage. After checking in, the porter escorted them to their room. It was the penthouse suite.

"Nico," she hissed after the porter closed the front door behind him. "Why did you get something this big?"

"What?" he laughed as he fell lazily onto the plush couch, swiping the remote off the leather ottoman. "I have instructions and a black card, to put you in the finest on your performance trips."

"We are only here for one night," she tried to reason with him, but he was already focused on the TV. "Were you able to get a hold of Mikhail?"

Misha had been worried about the lack of his call for the better part of the day. Even when her phone was still alive, she wasn't able to reach him by call or by text.

"Sort of," he mumbled. "He texted me back confirming everything."

Now she was very confused. But she wouldn't let herself think negatively or panic about it. Mikhail was probably just super busy. She would see him tomorrow and everything will be fine.

"Ok, then I am going to pick one of these three rooms and go take a shower." A mumble was the reply she received.

Picking the master suite, she walked into the large room with the equally large bed. Dear God, she was tired, the bed looked so soft and inviting all she wanted to do was say screw the shower and curl up on it. But she resisted. Hanging up her only dress bag in the grand empty walk in closet. With all her toiletries scattered on the bathroom counter, she laid her underwear and night clothes on the bed. Stepping into the shower, Misha took her time making sure to use all the soft, fragrant soaps and mousses provided. The bathroom was nice and fogged when she got out of the steamy shower. Wrapping a towel around her, she began to apply the lotion to her legs. A loud creaking noise paused her. Taking the shower cap off her head and clutching her towel tighter she peeked her head out of the bathroom door. Her room was pitch black. She was sure she left the lamp by the bed on. There was very little light streaming through the open curtains, and her eyes had yet to adjust to the darkness.

"Nico?" she called out.

"No, just me." The familiar deep voice caused her to jump. Before her eyes could process, a shape in the darkness quickly came forward and grabbed her by the arm pulling her out of the bathroom. Her bare feet stumbled over the plush carpet in her dark room as she fell against the strong, tall figure.

"Mikhail!" she screeched as she fell herself being lifted and dropped onto the bed. Thankfully she still managed to keep the towel clutched tightly over her breast. Her legs were a different story. She could feel the cold air whoosh up and between to her hot center as she tried to sit up on the soft bed. But strong hands gripped her thighs keeping them spread apart.

"So when you say you will never leave me, and I come home the next morning to find you have flown off with one of my men, leaves me very confused Misha." his gravely tone held a lethal edge.

The little bit of city light filtering through the gauzy hotel curtains only gave her his silhouette. The tall, powerful figure climbed further onto the bed pushing her legs even farther apart until he was kneeling directly between her legs. She never felt so exposed.

"I tried to call you," she began. But one of his hands grabbed at the plush towel before violently yanking away from her leaving her completely naked and spread open.

"And when I do get here," his rumbling voice continued as if he never heard her. "I find you sharing a room with Nico, your underwear laid proactively on the bed while your prancing around your room naked," he ground out the last words.

By now Misha was shaking in fear. His voice seemed so scary and the glimpses of his face through the night lights she could see flashes of his cold blue eyes. The grips on her thighs slid to the back of her knees pushing them up and forward. Her heart pounded as her most private areas were spread an exposed. But even though she was scared she could feel her pussy ache with hot tingling need.

"Mikhail you can't think that," she pleaded. "You know I only love you, and I am in my own room."

He didn't respond. Shifting he let her left leg drape over his large hot shoulder while his free hand began to lightly stroke her mounds.

"Oh!" she cried softly. It was so good. The feeling of his rough fingers gliding over her folds was killing her. "Please Mikhail," she begged.

Leaning forward until his face was inches from hers. "Never leave me again Misha."

The stroking stopped until she replied. "Yes. Yes, I am sorry," she rushed frantically. "I will ask you first."

A primal satisfaction seemed to pass over his arctic gaze. His large fingers roughly rubbed over her clit causing her to cry out in need.

"God," he whispered hoarsely as he began to quickly snatch off his shirt before he returned back to rubbing her throbbing clit. "You have no idea how long I have waited for this."

She was nearly out of her mind, Misha could barely hear him between the frustratingly light touches. But she did feel the scrape of his stubble on the inner part of her thigh as he trailed his surprisingly sharp teeth on the soft flesh of her thigh. Her whole body reacted to his sensuously dangerous touch as his mouth went lower and lower.

"I have drove myself from the brink of insanity holding myself back from you," his face was now inches from her folds. "and now I am going to take you in full."

Her mind barely had time to register what was happening until she felt his hot lips press against her most intimate flesh. Her alarmed cry went unheeded as his lips moved to the top of her slit, pinpointing the tiny bundle as he pushed her knee onto his shoulder higher as his tongue delved deep within her.

Her moans were ragged from the overwhelming pleasure. Never in her life did she imagine this. That he would do this to her. The feeling was so engulfing she had no idea what to do. She felt as if she was being consumed.

Black dots formed around the edges of her vision as she caught glimpses of his head buried between her legs, she felt any moment she would black out. His occasional nip at her sensitive clit would jolt another scream out of her demanding her to be all too aware of his exquisite torture.

Just as her body began to tighten and the wounding feeling threatened to break her, he stopped. With a cry of dismay, she pushed herself up from the tangle of sheets and pillows.

"Wha..." she feared he was leaving her like last time. Standing at the edge of the bed Mikhail removed the rest of his clothes in swift, easy movements. His eyes never left hers. The intensity of his bright blue yes made her body weep for more. She could swear his eyes were glowing in the dark room. He came back towards her filling the room with dark, lean male authority. Misha felt the hot skin of his thighs come in contact with hers before she felt his equally scorching kiss.

Instinctively she wrapped her legs around his strong hips as his mouth moved hungrily against hers. With both arms she clung to his powerful body. She could feel his hard length probe at her warm entrance.

Mikhail gave her no time to tense. She cried out as their bodies connected, the sharp pain as he stretched her took away her breath. Hesitantly she looked up into his eyes, for the longest moment they just stared at each other while his hips lay perfectly still between her legs. His muscular arms didn't waver as he lowered himself to her lips. It was the softest kiss she has ever known, slow and coaxing. Between the overwhelming feeling of being completely filled by this man and his tender kiss her whole body began to ache. Letting out a small moan she shifted underneath his weight.

Misha could feel him growl out a curse against her lips. Pushing himself up like a push up he let his hips rock forward. She cried out in pure ecstasy as he somehow settled deeper. Though he was already pulling out and pushing in again before she could acclimate. This time, her moan was smaller, since her body was adjusting around his cock, but he wasn't satisfied with that. Without warning he pulled back and thrusted in. Her ragged cry seemed to ignite something truly dark and hungry within him. Misha grasped at his shoulders as he grabbed both of her legs underneath her knees. She looked up in confused fear as he pushed her already aching legs higher to her chest. He smiled. A mean provoking smile as he slammed back into her. He rocked her and the bed violently as his hips matched the pace to her screams. Faintly she could hear herself begging him.

To stop or to continue she didn't know.

Her body seemed to have wound up tightly and exploded multiple times, but Mikhail did not stop. He buried his face in her breast before letting out a hoarse shout. After a long while drifting in and out of consciousness she felt herself being gathered close into strong arms. His heat surrounded her lulling her to sleep.

Chapter 24

A part of her was almost too afraid to open her eyes the next morning. What if everything went back to normal? What if Mikhail changed his mind?

The squeeze on her left ass cheek let her know he was awake. But it was the large calloused hand snaking over her hips that erased her worries. Misha could feel his rough fingers glide across the crisp curls between her thighs.

"Oh," she couldn't stop the moan from escaping her lips as she felt his fingers delve deeper.

"I could spend the entire day in bed with you," his voice was deep at the back of her head. "But we got to go, our plane leaves in an hour and Nico is already downstairs with the car."

She didn't even think of Nico. After everything that happened last night and now leaving the room together this morning. How will Nico react? Better yet, how will everyone react?

But nothing came of her worries. Nico was casual and laid back as usual when the drove to the airport. Though in truth Misha hardly could take note if any of Nico's reactions, she was too busy basking in Mikhail's attentions. It was as if a whole new door was opened. Of course, he was still very stoic for the most part but his proximity changed. On the plane he purposely pushed away the divider in their first class seats allowing him to pull her closer. There was an air of undeniable possessiveness that permeated around her when they dined at the Rose that night, in celebration of her performance. At first, she could sense Krill's hesitations but eventually subsided. Everything was clicking together perfectly.

Nothing however compared to their nights at home together. Sometimes it started with their rides home together. Sometimes it was just a glance from her or a kiss that went deeper than expected but it always ended up the same. Mikhail would break every traffic law to get home. The moment they were on their private elevator to the condo, he was undressing her. With her clothes scattered on the elevator floor, she was completely naked pressed up against the mirrored wall. With her ass partially perched on the railing, she wrapped her legs around his narrow torso. Mikhail's deep kiss never broke when the elevator chimed and opened on their floor. Even when he stopped to unlock the door, he pulled her closer, deepening the kiss.

There really wasn't a place they hadn't made love in their condo. It had been weeks since the night at the hotel in New York, and Mikhail's hunger for her has yet to diminish. With four powerful strides he had her pressed against the back of the couch. Grabbing at his buckle, she quickly undid the clasp. Her hands were not as shaky this time compared to the first time she initiated this. But Mikhail's didn't make her feel embarrassed actually quite the opposite. When she looked up at him to see if he noticed her nerves, she quickly inhaled. His blue eyes were dark with unreleased need it seemed her nervousness was only fanning the flames. Even now as he snatched off his shirt, ripping off a couple of buttons along the way, he seemed to be at his limit of his control.

Just as she was wrapping her arms around his neck to pull him closer, he pulled away. Stepping back, Mikhail gave her an unreadable smirk before quickly turning her over.

"Oh," she cried out in shock as the back of the sofa was now pressed against her stomach and her ass was high in the air. For some reason a wave of deep modesty hit her this position. She couldn't think of a time in the past few where Mikhail had access to her in this bent position. The feeling was overwhelming, embarrassment and arousal seemed to heat her body like flames. Teetering precariously she tried to reach behind her and shield herself from his view, but he wouldn't have it. Pushing her hands away, he gripped the curve of her hips and pulled her out slightly. Misha's eyes went wide as she felt the tip of his cock brush against her cheek as her feet dangled above the floor.

"You have no idea how long I have been dreaming of this." his voice was so deep and rough, Misha couldn't decide what was making her wetter his voice or the feeling of both of his large hands squeezing each cheek.

"I used to watch you walk this fat ass right by me wearing only one of my shirts, I nearly raped you then. I could just see myself fucking you on your hands and knees on the goddamn floor."

By now his words at her panting. Every now and then he would brush his thumb across her clit before going back to kneading her ass. With each squeeze of her ass, she could feel her cheeks being spread apart giving him his a full view.

Again she tried to cover herself. "Mikhail please," she begged. "You can see my..." Though she was so aroused, she was nearly crying she still couldn't bring herself to say anus.

A deep dark laugh was his response before spreading her ass further. "Don't worry my sweet, not now but soon we will explore this too."

Fear lanced through her at his words, but it was the feel of his finger grazing the puckered hole that made her cry out. However, her cry was cut off with a deep grunt as she felt her pussy being stretched. Thick fingers bit into her hips for purchase as he pulled himself back out to the tip. Exhaling heavily as the shock of his invasion, she let out another scream as he roughly thrust back in. It was not a slow love making like the times before. Instead, of slow, powerful thrust rocking in time with her body it was rough and hard, pulling her body to meet his needs.

Misha clutched onto the cushions as her body was wracked with convulsions of pleasure. The pleasure was so intense it was almost painful. She tried to call out for him to slow down. But in this position she was powerless. As the next convulsions took her, she felt her vision black out. The only this she remembered was his hoarse shout of release before falling heavily on top of her.

Hours later she woke up in his room pressed firmly against his hard chest. Blinking a couple of times, she felt him shift. Snuggling closer she could feel his heart beat thump strongly in his chest. Slowly she looked up and wasn't surprised to find him awake. She wanted to say something, but she didn't know what. Everything was just so perfect she didn't want to take a chance and destroy this moment.

"We need to get a new place," he stated flatly.

Shocked she leaned back to get a better look at him and to make sure she wasn't hearing things. "What. Why?"

"I feel like a fucking pedophile reliving fantasies in this damn place." he frowned at her as if she was making him do those things.

Laughing softly, she began to massage his large chest idly before speaking. "I have to admit I have been reliving quite a few myself."

"Have you?" he coaxed deeply while his free hand glided over her body.

"Remember the night a long time ago. Well, you probably don't remember, but you gave me some of your drink when I had trouble sleeping."

"The hell if I don't remember that," he let his thumb rest heavily on her nipple. The simple act made her throb. Leaning down, he captured her lips in a hot slow kiss bringing her closer to him. Feeling his hot length against her stomach, she swallowed hard. "God I bet you don't remember what you said to me that night?"

"What?" She didn't remember saying anything.

"You said you wished you were the woman in my bed that night."

"Oh my God."

"Yeah it nearly killed me," he grumbled still obviously frustrated from her words years ago. "From that to you telling me you love me every day, and you undressing me with your eyes every damn day. I'm proud of myself I held back for this long."

Laughing she snuggled in closer to his heat. His large body seemed to radiate so much heat she had to fight off the lull of sleep. How could she be sleepy when he just mentioned getting a new place together. Her heart swelled at the permanence of his words alluded to. Please God, she hoped this lasted forever. But she didn't want to just hope.

A few minutes ticked by as she internally wrestled with her doubt. She wanted to just ask him point blankly, but what if she reached the moment. Or worse ruined everything. What if her asking him is the same mistake all the other women before her made? Now the swelling in her heart to a clenching vice.

"Ok what are you thinking?" he asked she could hear the frown in his voice.

"What?" No, I was..." she tried to make her voice light and playful, but she failed miserably.

"Misha," his unspoken command did not go unnoticed in the simple statement of her name. "Your whole body went from soft to tense, and I can feel you eyelashes blinking against me. What are you thinking?" He pushed her away from him just far enough so he could look her in the eye. For the first time in all the years living with the silent criminal, he looked unsure.

"Are you having second thoughts," he paused, the grip on her shoulders tightened.

"No, no of course not," she rushed to reply. "It's just that, I was just thinking," God now the words were getting twisted in her head from fear.

Taking a deep breath she continued.

"I'm scared that you might grow tired of me. I mean what can I do differently that your girlfriends in the past could not do."

"Girlfriends?" Mikhail's eyebrows furrowed together in confusion as he stared at her before relaxing in clarity. "I see."

Mikhail sat up in the bed and for a second of pure panic she thought he was leaving, instinctively she grabbed his arm. Looking at her hand and her fear stricken face Mikhail paused before sighing in what seemed to be disappointed.

Quickly letting go of his arm Misha grabbed the covers to get up as well, she needed to apologize. The whole mood was ruined, and she was the cause.

Propping himself against the headboard he pulled her into his lap just as he did the other night. Pushing her tangled hair out of the way with one hand she clutched the sheet to her breast with the other.

With their faces inches apart Mikhail gave her a self-depreciating smile.

"I am not proud to say that all the women that I have been with have been paid in one way or another."

He paused letting the information sink in.

"All of them?"

He did not respond to the question. "I know I have everything working against me Misha. My past, my career choice, the fact that I have never been in any meaningful relationship. Before I meet you, I never knew what love felt like. Of course, you hear about it but I never believed in it. I probably would have experienced it if I wasn't robbed of my sister." his grip around her tightened. "But then one day a little girl comes into my life and tells me every day for over nine years straight that she loves me. And the by some cruel twist of fate I became infatuated with you. I was actually afraid I would somehow fuck things up, so I distanced myself. But that nearly made things worse. I finally came to terms with it my sweet little Misha. I'm scared shitless because I love you very much. I have never felt anything this fucking great and debilitating at the same time. Please believe me then I tell you I want to spend the rest of my life with you."

Somewhere along the way she started crying. Wrapping her arms around his neck she pulled herself close, feeling his arms wrap around her in kind. It seems for so long they were both lost one way or another but now they were found.

Fin

Thank you,

I hope you enjoyed it. Please feel free to leave me *five shiny* stars as a review.

Katerina Winters

Check out my other book: Glass Cage:

After her mother's untimely death, finishing school was no longer an option for Christelle DeMelo.

A chance job offering led her into the cruel hands of Alexei Petrov. On the outside, the stoic Russian appeared to be a normal wealthy businessman who needed a maid to keep up with his particular demands. However, Christelle knows the real man, the monster in an expensive suit. Her and her infant brother's livelihood depend on the tall amber eyed criminal who wants nothing more than her complete obedience.

From the moment he laid eyes on her Alexei had every intention to possess his innocent maid. But when she arrived at his door one night carrying her brother and a black eye Alexei happily threw out his initial plans for a slow seduction. Seizing the opportunity Alexei presented her with a deal she had no choice to accept.

Made in the USA
Monee, IL
23 June 2021